MW00626717

The Mistletoe Paradox

A Monday Night Anthology

LIZ LEO
KRISTINA HORNER
KATRINA HAMILTON
SUNNY EVERSON
JENNIFER LEE SWAGERT
MARIA BEREJAN
STEPHEN FOLKINS
SHAY LYNAM
RACHAEL STERLING

These are works of fiction. Names, characters, places, and incidents either are the product of the authors' imagination or are used fictitiously. Any resemblance to actual persons, living or dead, events, or locales is entirely coincidental.

"Signing Off" copyright © 2021 by Liz Leo
"Spin the Bottle" copyright © 2021 by Kristina Horner
"Cultivate" copyright © 2021 by Katrina Hamilton
"Rewind" copyright © 2021 by Sunny Everson
"Trusty Milo™'s Original Merry Mistletoe Moonshine for Authentic Holiday Cheer" copyright © 2021 by Jennifer Lee Swagert
"The Longest Night" copyright © 2021 by Maria Berejan
"To Give and To Receive" copyright © 2021 by Stephen Folkins
"Snowball Fights and Thursday Nights" copyright © 2021 by Shay Lynam
"Mandatory Nondenominational Socialization Event" copyright © 2021 by Rachael Sterling

All rights reserved. No part of this book may be reproduced or used in any manner without written permission of the copyright owner except for the use of quotations in a book review.

Published by 84th Street Press.
Address: 84thstreetpress@gmail.com.
Visit us on the Web! www.84thstreetpress.com

First paperback edition November 2021 printed in Seattle, WA, USA

Cover by Adam Levermore
Editing by Morgan Wegner

ISBN 978-1-956273-03-8 (paperback)
ISBN 978-1-956273-04-5 (hardcover)
ISBN 978-1-956273-05-2 (ebook)
Library of Congress Control Number: 2021922358

The Mistletoe Paradox

A Monday Night Anthology

LIZ LEO
KRISTINA HORNER
KATRINA HAMILTON
SUNNY EVERSON
JENNIFER LEE SWAGERT
MARIA BEREJAN
STEPHEN FOLKINS
SHAY LYNAM
RACHAEL STERLING

Table of Contents

Dedication

Dedicated to The Rev. Eston Collins
Thank you for recognizing and believing in young
writers

The Prompt

Write a story inspired by the phrase "The Mistletoe Paradox" within a single four-hour sitting.

———

The Anthology

The Monday Night Anthology series began with a single prompt.

The prompt itself was not particularly important; the idea that grew from it was. At the point we stumbled upon it, we had been writers in a writing group meeting once a week for over four years. Yet in that time, we'd never written anything together — at least not in the form of a joint project. But then we stumbled on a prompt, and as we talked about it, we realized we each had ideas for a story. We got excited, and as often happens, the excitement became infectious.

So, one adventurous November day, our writing group decided to sit down and write this story — each person's interpretation of it. We shared small snippets during writing breaks, laughing at quirky lines over meatballs and cake, but mostly we kept our ideas guarded until we were done. Later, we critiqued the stories, and we were left astounded by how imaginative and wildly different each idea and each author's writing style was.

We decided to recreate this experiment with a new prompt: "The Mistletoe Paradox." Once more we sat down and wrote, and then eagerly critiqued each other's work. And once more the results floored us. Genres, characters, and points of view varied; some stories were uplifting, some were dark; some comedic, some horrifying; some set worlds away, others in worlds past. It was hard to believe they had all come from the same small nugget of an idea. Above all else, they *fit* each other in a special way that, when read together, showcased the uniqueness of each story.

We knew we were onto something special with these projects. Creating together in this way — and seeing these results — was a thrill unlike anything we'd previously shared as a writing group. We knew, then and there, that we had to continue.

Thus, the Monday Night Anthology series began.

———

More Monday Night Anthologies

Boys, Book Clubs, and Other Bad Ideas

Signing Off

by Liz Leo

Captain's Log - 8.12.3408 - Parallel 41
SS Mistletoe
Captain Janterra Lancing

Brill told me I have to keep a captain's log. So here we go.

———

Captain's log kept.

Captain's Log - 8.13.3408 - Parallel 41
SS Mistletoe
Captain Janterra Lancing

Brill informed me that I actually have to log things in the captain's log.

He wouldn't tell me what I was supposed to log, exactly, so I suppose I have to make another clumsy attempt before he lobs more criticism at me.

Maybe I'll log what a real rebar in the gasket Brill is. I'll log how he sticks his nose up at everything, and nothing is good enough for him. And how he wouldn't let me name my own star-swearing ship. And when I asked why, he said it's because I'm not clever.

3

Then I said, "I am plenty clever."

And he said, "Name a time you were clever, then."

And I couldn't come up with anything on the spot.

So he named it the *Starship Mistletoe*.

He said it's because of this plant called *Mistletoe*. A parasitic shrub that lives off of trees, sucking them of nutrients and hydration. He said it was clever because we're a leeching vessel that attaches onto unsuspecting cruisers for fuel and anything Linea can cart into our cargo hold.

Is that what being clever is? Making a parallel between two things that no one even cares about?

Because I can do that. Remember when I called Brill a real rebar in the gasket? That's a parallel between two things that no one cares about. Brill and gaskets.

Captain's Log - 10.17.3408 - Parallel 41
SS Mistletoe
Captain Janterra Lancing

Brill now informs me that I have to log more things than talking about what a block in the respiration tube he is. He also informed me that I have to write in this log at least once a month. I asked Brill if he wanted to be captain and I would control operations instead, but he told me that if I were in charge of operations, I would probably run the ship into the ground, and I couldn't argue with that because when I picked him

4

up on Felsaur 9 I *had* run the ship into the ground, and that's why I hired him on as head of operations.

Linea is here too. It's nice to have another girl on the ship, even though she isn't really interested in my relationship problems or what color I should hydro-dye my hair next. She's the...well, I never gave her a title when we brought her on. She...schleps things. You know. Cargo. Fuel. Food. *Things*. She brings them from point A to point B. Point A usually being the massive cruiser we're attached to. And Point B being the *SS Mistletoe* (still think it's a dumb name if you're reading this, Brill).

———

I've been running the ship for a year now. Feels like longer. And shorter. Longer and shorter at the same time. Like in the space of time when you're waiting outside a medic's office to be called in. That limbo where you've been sitting there forever, but also you don't want to have to face the reality that the space ticks that you picked up at a bar on Felsaur 9 aren't coming off without an intrusively painful and excessively expensive procedure.

I got the ship when I turned 19.

Sort of a birthday gift.

From myself.

To myself.

You know how every little girl grows up waiting for her mommy and daddy to give her a shiny red starship for her 19th birthday? Well, my mommy was a test tube from Felsaur 8, and my daddy was a clone center on Barrelon, so I had to make my own dreams happen.

When I saw what would soon become the *SS Mistletoe* sitting there curbside outside the emergency medical clinic, bright and shiny and red, I knew I had to have her. My ex was the type of wealthy that led him astray for a year or two after he graduated, so naturally he was the one who taught me how to hotwire a ship. Funny thing—like most people that rich, he didn't have to be adrift for too long. He got to go back to luxury, and I had to keep on leeching well after he was gone.

The galaxies are full of dumb giant whales—these massive starliners and cruisers that we latch onto and loot when we get low on supplies. My ship cloaks well. We slide in all easy and silent, mostly because the *Mistletoe* has auto-docking, and the whales and their crew never even notice.

You know what they say: If it's not bolted down, it belongs to the stars.

Captain's Log 11.20.3408 - Parallel 41
SS Mistletoe
Captain Janterra Lancing

More notes from Brill:
1. Stop incriminating yourself in your stolen ship's blackbox.

6

2. A captain's log is about logging what happened that day, not jabbering on about the past.

———

So, what happened today? Is that what I'm supposed to write about?

Brill ate a worm.

I wasn't going to *not* write about it, Brill. You told me to talk about what happened, and that's what happened today.

We docked on a large, drab-green cruiser. While Brill and I pumped fuel, Linea pried open the airlock, got herself into the cargo bay, and came back with a few loads labeled "*f. supplies.*"

"F for 'food,' surely," I announced.

We had been a bit too long between gigs, so we hadn't swiped much to eat lately. We opened those boxes like it was Christmas morning. They were stocked with neatly sealed plastic cartons of all sorts of brightly colored shapes. Looked like candy. *Looked like it.*

Brill broke one open and dumped the contents right into his all-but-unhinged jaw without even paying attention to what he was inhaling. To be completely honest, the only reason I hadn't beaten him to it was because I was having trouble unwrapping my own box of mystery food items.

Then Brill choked and sputtered. He turned near purple in the face and spat out a whole mouthful of bright grubs, which were wiggling as much as he was.

Turns out the whale was a research vessel. Marine. Headed to Aquantis for an expedition. We'd managed to nab a metric tonne of fishing bait.

Some of it was actually edible, once we cooked it over a blaster pipe.

But not the worms, Brill. Not the worms.

So that is what is going to be eternally recorded now for anyone who comes across this in the future, or past, to read.

Captain's Log 12.22.3408 - Parallel 41
SS Mistletoe
Captain Janterra Lancing

Today *he* called.

———

Brill told me not to pick up. Brill has a habit of always being right about these things. I dislike it because I have the equal but opposite habit of always being wrong about these things. But there is something about seeing your ex's call sign pop up on the dashboard that just makes your brains liquify and flow out your butt. I told Brill that *I* was captain, so I was going to make all the bad decisions I wanted.

I brought *him* up on the holo-screen and I made the best pose I could in my captain's chair: legs crossed, elbow on the armrest, hair swept back behind me so he couldn't see the tangles. I puffed out my chest a bit so he might have thought that in the last six months my figure had filled out in all the areas he had regularly criticized. I subtly flicked the switch on my armrest that enabled a holo-filter to smooth out my skin so that he wouldn't see the bags under my eyes.

"Jan! You're looking well!" he exclaimed from the captain's deck of a military star liner. His voice was big and full of the boom of unadulterated promise. It always had been like that when he talked to me.

"And you," I told him. I made sure not to use his name. As if he was so insignificant to me that I might have managed to misplace it in the hubbub of my marauding lifestyle.

"You know why I called, don't you?" His tone slowed so that he could seem sweet. "Seeming" was all he ever needed. In flashes of memory, I could hear different words in the same tone.

"You can read a star map, can't you?"

"You're doing this just to annoy me, aren't you?"

"You know why I'm leaving you, don't you?"

"Of course," I told him. Although I didn't. I never did.

"Then you know what I'm going to say next, right?" His dark hair was swirled up in a robust curl at the crown of his head. His teeth were white and perfectly aligned, like the input valves on the side of a military-grade galaxy launcher.

"I do." I still didn't.

"Then why don't you save me having to say it." He leaned on his liner's navigation controls, clad in a perfectly pressed, navy-blue suit, like he didn't have a care in the cosmos.

And I'd be surprised if he did.

He was born from money. His parents weren't rich when they had him, no, but it was his birth that made them the second most wealthy family in the universe. His mother was on an antipsychotic pharmaceutical that, while in the process of childbirth, turned her invisible. They sued and won the largest settlement in the history of all of space and time, and their lawyer was paid enough to afford a mansion on Felsaur 7. His mother remained invisible, but I've met her, and I can assure you she doesn't mind.

Hell, I'd be invisible, too, for that kind of money.

We met at a bar—the same bar where I got space ticks. But a different night.

We were both right out of school—him a fancy prep institute; me a juvenile detention center. He had all the money in the universe. I had all the optimism in the universe.

I loved his smile, bright and shining like the third moon on Felsaur 6. And the way he knew so much about life, even though we were the same age. Through his riches he had lived what felt like the equivalent of a thousand normal lifetimes. He taught me how to steal anything my heart desired. How to make out in the back of the opera house without anyone noticing by using a time suspension bubble. How to fall in love. And, eventually, how to fall out of it.

"Jan?"

I tried to buy myself some time by switching poses on my captain's chair. However, the move served to rip the back of my jumpsuit with a sound probably transmittable via the ship's conference system.

"Mm-hmm?" I replied.

"I don't want to have to say it."

"Say what?" I batted my eyelashes, in case that would help somehow.

"That you're trespassing in a restricted military licensed quadrant, the penalty for which is five years imprisonment and a fine of twenty thousand credits. You've never really been good with navigation, have you, Jan?"

I shook my head and tried to keep my eyes open wide and unassuming. I wish I had put on makeup, or done my hair, or fixed any of the various rips and burns in my jumpsuit.

"I'm letting you know now, as a personal favor." That smile. Those teeth. Like a row of white missile caps pointed right at you, locked on target, ready to fire.

"How...kind of you." I used to love the way he would dote on me with favors I never asked for in the first place.

"I just hope you're doing well, Jan." His pose on the screen was effortlessly handsome. I started to remember what it felt like to be in his arms. To have him shine promises upon me with the same fervor as an arching solar flare. To feel the infinite possibilities that being with him allowed.

"Oh, I'm doing well," I told him. *Am I? I'm still leeching. Our last haul was fishing bait. I was seconds away from eating worms.* "Really, really well."

"I'm glad to hear that. You know..." — there was a pause in which I began to see that flash of infinity again — "there's a battalion gala coming up in a week. I haven't chosen who I'm inviting as the ol' plus-one. They're raising money to bulk up their security systems. How much fun would it be if I brought a leecher?"

He laughed at his own joke.

I laughed, too. Not a real laugh, but a parasitic laugh that can only exist if attached to a first, more robust laugh.

"So, what do you say, Jan?" He winked at me.

I hadn't seen him wink at me since before we split. It sparked something in me like a carburetor turning an engine. My heart rumbled, full of gasoline and smoke.

"You're not serious," I spluttered. It had to be one of his signature jokes at my expense. He always liked to joke, after all. That's where that multiverse of potential came from. You never knew what he would settle on. He was always a coin caught in the falling between heads and tails. If the coin never fell, you'd always feel like you were going to win the toss.

"Try me," he grinned. "I like making waves. Surely you remember that. Do you have a dress? Something formal, black tie, nicer than the usual...You know what? I'll send you something." The last phrase was clearly said after he took a hard look at my jumpsuit's current state of affairs.

"I dunno." I was put off guard again. If this was a game of starball, he was already over my forward boundary and heading for the goal. "I'll have to check my calendar."

I didn't have a calendar.

"Since when do you have a calendar?" His eyes were starry with delight.

"I keep a captain's log, too." It wasn't a well-prepared defense, but it was all I could think to say.

"Well, look at Jan, all grown up now, huh? Well then, consult your calendar, and while you're at it, make sure to get yourself out of this restricted zone, alright? Don't want the hammer of the enforcer squadron coming down on you and ruining your hair before next Sunday."

"Sunday. Gotcha." I nodded. "I'll…call you back if I can make it."

"Schrodinger's date, then." He winked again. A *second* wink.

And then he signed off.

———

I turned around to see Brill and Linea, witnesses to the entire exchange, staring at me with eyes wider than a spaceball goalpost.

"You can*not* go." Brill almost tripped over his rolled-up jumpsuit hem running up to me.

"Doesn't matter what you say," Linea shrugged. "She's going to say yes."

"That was a star-swearing disaster," Brill continued. "I wanted to die for you, it was so bad."

"It wasn't *that* bad, was it?" I looked to Linea for support.

She nodded slowly and solemnly, like a parent telling her child that her parrot-puppy needed to be put down.

"It was rough," Linea admitted.

"That's the problem." Brill started walking back to his post on the starboard side of the ship. "He has always had all the power in this. You're just a little solar ant following the magma-sugar crumbs he leaves for you."

"Eat a worm, Brill," I told him, and slammed my fist down on the controls, jumping us out of the quadrant and into somewhere new. I didn't care where, really. It didn't matter. All that mattered was that I had been a complete and utter buffoon in the face of my ex-boyfriend, and to make matters worse, he had the gall to try to ask me out.

But the worst thing of all?

I was actually considering saying yes.

Captain's Log 12.23.3429 - Parallel 42
SS Mistletoe
Captain Janterra Lancing

Immediately following the writing of my last captain's log, and without an answer to the question of whether I should attend the gala or not, I decided to drink.

For twelve hours.

I drank for long enough that Brill and Linea joined in and out over the course of my mislaid revelry, the way you might check into a hotel on Felsaur 5 for vacation on Friday and then go back to normal life on the following Monday.

I drank like peach schnapps was my career. Like I had gone to vocational school for peach schnapps. Like peach schnapps was paying me a pension.

I retired in the lavatory for a long while after that, firmly attached to the commode, deeply questioning my life choices.

Then I spent the next two hours rolling around my bunk trying to sleep and doing about as good a job as I did navigating my ship.

And it wasn't until another hour later, dehydrated coffee in hand, that I chanced a look at where our ship had jumped.

Normally the controls to jump parallels are locked—in most standard-issue models, at least. But opening up the ship's chassis to hotwire it must've undone all of the basic settings. It more or less put the operating system into sandbox mode. Another reason no alerts triggered when we wandered into illegal territory once before.

Where we trespassed yesterday was criminal.

Where we ended up today is forbidden.

Strangely, we kept in the same rough X, Y, and Z coordinates, but jumped give-or-take twenty years in the future and shifted one parallel down.

There are lots of reasons they teach you in grade school about why it's banned to jump parallels. Universes are a lot like bathtubs. When you get into a bathtub, the water level rises, but hopefully never above the ledge.

However, if you tried to get into a bathtub that a version of you was already in, it would certainly overflow as you both awkwardly tried to fit into the same small, wet space. So, some objects from the parallel universe you arrived in would be splashed into the parallel universe you left, like rubber duckies riding on the bubbles.

The problem being, of course, that you could not return to the universe you had just come from for around 24 hours, until the water evened out and the ripples calmed. And by then, it would be hard to tell what damage had been done.

———

I have decided not to tell Brill and Linea.

They don't need to know. After all, that's what a captain's log is for, right? A place to note important matters—like accidentally traveling into a forbidden dimension—and then close the book and go on with your life.

A place to put all the things that happened so that you don't have to really think about them any more after that. Sort of like a trash chute for your thoughts.

I'm pretty sure we can just wait out our 24 hours peacefully, avoid contacting any other ships, and then head back home.

Nothing will happen, and that will be that.

Captain's Log 12.24.3429 - Parallel 42
SS Mistletoe
Captain Janterra Lancing

Something happened.

———

I thought we could do it. Just 24 hours of laying low. Even if a really big and tasty-looking whale swam by, I could convince Brill and Linea to hold off until I was feeling better.

But then the biggest, brightest, most *rob-able* starship came into our orbit. Although it's more likely we were swung into its orbit, as it was about the size of a small moon.

It was even shaped a bit like a moon: long, crescent, and lined with platinum sheets so that any and every light that washed upon it lit up the vessel in gleaming brilliance. It was so abhorrently opulent that you would have had to be *mad* to ignore it.

———

We locked onto the larger ship just like normal, with Linea getting ready to schlep, Brill getting ready to disarm any alarm systems, and me pressing the "auto-dock" button.

But when we got inside, a feeling of acidic unease pulsed from my stomach and up my esophagus to arrive bitterly in my throat. To start, the cargo bay had nothing in it. These large ships *always* had some sort of excess in their holds. A recent delivery. An overflow of stock. But these were pristine, white-walled vaults of nothingness.

Totally empty.

"Imagine being so rich you had a ship that's the size of a small planet and nothing in your cargo hold?" Linea complained.

"I say we go deeper," I urged. True, I hadn't wanted to go on board the ship initially. But once we docked, I didn't see the harm in pushing our boundaries just a little more. I needed a reward to justify our recklessness.

"What do you think this type of ship is for?" Brill asked as we exited the airlock into the bowels of the vessel. The walls were made of polished marble; the floors, silver-mirrored tiles. "Post-post-postmodern art gallery?"

"Wonder why there wasn't an alarm." I was amazed by the silence that permeated the halls. The cold walls should have at least echoed our steps, but

18

instead they absorbed the noise. Despite the fact that there were three of us in our heavy jumpsuits, the only sound I could hear was something between a distant forest breeze and the trickle of a stream over pebbles.

And that is when I turned around, and Brill and Linea weren't behind me anymore.

I called out to them, but my voice didn't travel. Not to mention I should have been sweating in my suit, but instead I was as chilled as the ice-bears on Felsaur 4. Goosebumps rose on my neck.

I can't tell you why I didn't go back and look for them. Why I didn't run screaming all the way back to my ship.

But I think it had something to do with the fact that I smelled bacon.

I let the tantalizing scent guide me, twisting around the corridors, winding left and right, until I was finally let out at a simple door. I didn't even need to open it. It whooshed clear for me.

"I thought you said you'd be another week in the Barglast System, dear," a voice echoed throughout a structure as large as the Space-Pope's Cathedral. The voice sounded both big and small, the way a star that's lightyears away can look like a pinprick but also be so immense a solar system orbits it.

The room in front of me came in two parts. The first was a wide, arching set of windows that looked out into the deepness of space, hundreds of yards tall, creating a conservatory that existentially mimicked the way I often felt when contemplating the infinite nature of the universe right before falling asleep. It was clear, now, that the gleaming outer panels were not decoration, but simply the light hitting so many panes of tinted windows that I can't even think of a number to compare it to.

The second part of the room rested at its center, looking almost miniature, surrounded by the cavernous outer room.

The tiny room was a kitchen.

Well, half a kitchen.

The type of kitchen I used to watch in old holo-shows, with a sink basin to wash in, a fridge to keep food fresh, a table to eat around, and a burner to fry bacon. But the room consisted of only two walls, like a stage play set, or a home someone began to build and abandoned halfway through.

"You're just in time, though! I've cooked some breakfast for us," the woman called again, still absorbed in the crackling meat. She was wearing a dress as blue as an atmospheric sky, fitted in the bodice and flared past the waist. Her hair was curled in rolls and pinned to her head elegantly. "I made your favorite: bacon and —"

The woman turned around and the words left her.

Then the room left her as well.

The walls, the fridge — even the window with daisy-dotted curtains faded. So did the technicolor dress and perfect hair. The pan, spatula, and bacon disintegrated in her grip.

In front of me was a mature woman, perhaps in her forties, dressed in a simple white frock and gray pants, and whose hair, while braided back with effort, looked as if it were once wild and uncontrollable.

We were left standing in front of each other in an empty leviathan's belly.

"You're not my husband." The woman grasped at her arms like they were a life preserver that would help her float.

"I'm not." I nodded and took a step forward. She looked familiar. Like a photograph I'd seen in a tabloid headline, or on a wanted poster slapped on a truck stop bathroom door.

"How'd you get aboard my ship?" Her arms were still crossed. At first I had thought maybe she was nuts, a lunatic woman in a pretend world. But her eyes were fierce, dark, and narrowed. She was not soft. She was angry, but very practiced at holding it in.

"This is *your* ship?" I realized that my voice echoed widely in this room, as if all of the sound in the rest of the ship ended up here, keeping the hallways silent.

"Of course it is. Why would I be on it if it wasn't?"

She made a good point.

"I was lost"—the excuse would at least buy me time to think of a better answer—"so I docked to see if I could find some supplies. I didn't hear an alarm, so I figured you might be open to...visitors."

"I don't need an alarm." A muscle in the woman's left eye tensed as she spoke. "The *Willow* has a system that rejects anyone who doesn't match my or my husband's DNA. If anyone tries to enter, they're teleported right back to their ship."

That did set my mind at ease. Brill and Linea were safe on the *Mistletoe* and not, as in a worry that did briefly cross my mind, suspended in peril darker than the infinite cave system of Felsaur 3. But I was still aboard her ship, the *Willow*. Why hadn't I been booted, too?

"You're not one of his illegitimate children, are you? One of the ones his mother made me a brochure about when she was trying to convince me not to marry him?" As she took a few steps toward me, brushstrokes of color began to form behind her with each word. Rays of purple, splashes of indigo, a few teal splatters.

I shook my head. My father was synthetic DNA.

"Good, because I've always worried one might pop up one day asking to be made heir to his fortune. Do me a favor and never get a star-swearing fortune. More trouble than it's worth."

That's when I realized she had on a wedding ring, and it wasn't holographic. It was a diamond bigger than one of the hail rocks in a Felsaur 2 ice storm. Half of it could have made up the GDP of a small planet.

"You don't have to worry about me. I'm from a clone center. The only thing I inherited was a really bad sense of direction."

"Me too." The woman let herself drop a hint of a smile. I did not know if she meant that she, too, was a clone, or that she also had a really bad sense of direction.

A mahogany table materialized in front of her out of three-dimensional pixels. A chair pulled out and she sat down. I found myself doing the same.

"Must be lonely on this ship, all by yourself." I wanted to keep the conversation off of my trespassing for as long as I could.

"My husband's here," she explained, "although not as often as I'd like. He has business a lot of the time. Always traveling. Dentron for a work lunch. Luncet-Optora for a convention. Felsaur 1 for a board meeting. You'd think being the second richest person in the universe would mean you didn't have to work so much."

The wash of colors behind her darkened. Maroons into wine reds into deep browns into a color that matched the dark coffee that had appeared in front of me.

"Sorry he's gone a lot," I told her, sipping from the mug. "I sort of have the opposite problem. Someone that won't let me go. Or that I can't let go."

She nodded, also drinking from her cup, although from the pungent smell that found its way across the table the contents did not appear to be coffee, but some sort of strongly flavored alcohol.

"Do you need to let him go?" she asked, holding her cup up so that I could not see her expression, but I guessed she was smiling knowingly. Behind her the colors lightened. A golden pastiche swirled in ambiguous shapes.

"I dunno." I shrugged, setting down my mug. "I don't know how you ever know. Maybe you can tell me. You're in love, right? How do you make it work?"

She spent some time looking down at her cup, which refilled after each sip so that the level of liquid never lowered.

"Love is a bit like the wind." She lifted her gaze, but it didn't settle on me. Instead, she focused on something in the distance behind me.

I heard a door open.

She stood up from her seat, the wooden chair squeaking against the floor as she displaced herself.

"You can't see it." She walked past the table. A burgundy dress bloomed around her. Her hair was pulled into a graceful bun. "But you can feel it. So you harness its power. Glide on it. Dance in it."

I turned over my shoulder to see that a man had walked in through a freestanding door. He was dressed in a navy suit, brown hair slicked back, smile luminous against the darkening holographic stage. The lights lowered as they walked closer to each other, spotlights focused on each of them.

"But it wears down all your edges. Over years, it weathers everything into the path of least resistance." The woman held out a hand for the man to take. "And most of all —"

As her fingers were about to grasp his, he disappeared.

The scene lightened. The red dress fell from her like petals.

"There is no wind in space."

Alone with me again, she sat back down and sipped from her ever-filling cup.

"That's star-swearing bleak." I almost laughed, but thankfully stifled the instinct.

"Was it?" She shrugged and set down her cup, and then the cup was no more. "I didn't mean it to be."

"I think I need to get going." I stood up, and she did as well. The same impulse that drew me in was now telling me it was time to leave. "Get back to my ship."

"You could stay on the *Willow*." She stepped forward, and a meadow began to grow around her. Bare feet nestled in grass, frogs jumping from between blades. "For a while. Before he gets back." The sun rose behind her and cleared up the canvas of interwoven colors. Birds chirped. The breeze blew the smell of flowers toward me.

I wanted to ask her more questions. What was she doing, alone, in her own ship? Why wasn't she out exploring the universe, too? Why did she escape into these false memories instead of following him, or herself even, into new unknowns?

But considering her dark answer to my first question, I didn't want to take the chance.

"Thanks for not calling the authorities on me," I told her, finding my way back to the door. "And sorry your security system is busted."

She simply smiled and waved.

As I left, the meadow disappeared. The kitchen folded open upon the empty stage, her perfect housewife costume drawn over her blank form once again. The bacon began to fry.

Captain's Log 12.25.3408 - Parallel 41
SS Mistletoe
Captain Janterra Lancing

I think she might have been *me*.
And that he might have been *him*.

———

It took me longer than I'd like to admit to figure it out, but I don't think you can face yourself and know it. Not right away.

The same way you can't binge-drink peach schnapps and not be hungover the whole next day. Or how you can't get rid of space ticks with a miracle cure you found online. How you can't stop thinking about him even though you just *know* he's stopped thinking about you.

———

While I hadn't planned on telling my crew about jumping parallels, they deserved to know. And a captain's log is not the best place to keep things bottled up. A captain's log can't give you comfort when you have to see a future version of yourself

26

married to a future version of your ex-boyfriend. There is no sympathy in these pages. Just a lot of me, talking about myself, to me.

To Brill's credit, after he got done laughing at me, and to Linea's, after she got done doubting me, each of them gave me a steadfast hug. Then Linea put on my favorite album, Brill danced badly for my amusement, and we waited out the few hours left before we could jump home.

―――――

When we leapt back into 41, we arrived right in the middle of what I assumed was a meteor shower. Multiple thuds landed on the ship's hull, banging like we were under attack. But it turns out we had simply materialized amongst a sea of white, pristine cargo boxes. Enough to fill a whole cargo bay, even.

We got out on our leads, scooped them into sacks, and brought what we could catch into the ship. I noticed each box was marked with a crest. Painted on the alabaster metal in a fine, gray stencil was the silhouette of a willow tree.

When we took out a crowbar and lifted the tops, we were met with a bounty of the finest fuels, richest foods, crates of champagne, and the types of furs and sundries one might imagine only the second richest person in the universe could afford.

"This is a whole lot better than fish bait," Brill said. Linea agreed.

I hate to admit it, but Brill was *absolutely* right.

When they had exhausted themselves with merriment and fallen asleep, I remained on deck in the captain's chair, watching the dashboard as we continued to freefall into the dark, frictionless void in front of us.

I pulled up *his* call sign and watched as his static image floated above me in holographic glory. Even handsome in dimensional pixels. I could hear his voice in the echo of the rumble of my ship's engines. I remembered him telling me that he loved me. I wondered what he meant when he said it. Or if he meant nothing at all, like the wailing of the wind.

I flirted with the idea of pressing "call" and telling him that I would be his date to the gala. That he didn't need to mail me a gown because I had just found at least a dozen in the white cargo boxes that were — go figure — exactly my size. That I was excited to be in his arms again, even if only for one night.

But instead, I opened up his contact and, with as much certainty as I had when I originally button-mashed my way into another universe, I pressed "delete."

Our conversation logs vanished, and his image left my screen.

I popped open one last bottle of champagne to swig and, with just as much abandon, plotted my next course into the unknown.

Spin the Bottle

by Kristina Horner

"Holly, it's your turn!"

Gemma Harper wiped at her lipstick and rolled an empty champagne bottle my way. She had just finished *gratuitously* making out with Fletcher Harrison in front of her entire new circle of friends and was giving me a knowing look.

Instead of spinning, I rolled it back. "I pick Truth."

The circle groaned.

Gemma had invented the game and was quite proud of it: Picking "Dare" meant spinning the bottle. It saved our circle of horny teenagers the trouble of pretending they were here to do anything else.

"Truth" was…well, to be frank, it was for me. I told Gemma the only way I'd come to her Christmas party was if I had options. She replied that she'd invited at *least* six boys — but we both knew that wasn't what I meant. I'm not really the make-out-party type. I'm also not the secret-spilling type, but my choices were limited.

"Fine," Gemma sighed, standing the bottle upright in the middle of the circle. She'd nicked it from the party her parents had going on upstairs — a party that was shockingly much wilder than ours. She found her parents to be extremely embarrassing, but I appreciated grown-ups who still knew how to have fun. But then again, maybe it was just easier to appreciate parents that weren't your own.

Regardless, us teenagers were steering clear of the merriment on the main floor, which was easy enough to do with our ample amounts of hot cocoa, chocolate chip cookies, and hormones.

"Okay, Holly. Truth, then." Gemma raised an eyebrow at me. "Which boy do you want to kiss?"

"That's not fair," I whined, but the other kids in the circle were already making catcalls.

Gemma already *knew* the answer to this question. It was why she forced us to play this stupid game in the first place.

My eyes flitted to the left. Stuart Hobbs sat beside me with his legs crossed and his hands in his lap, and I couldn't help but notice he looked embarrassed, too.

Embarrassed for me? Embarrassed *of* me?

"Ooh," said Mindy, catching me looking. "It's Stuart, isn't it? Look at how she's looking at him."

My crush on Stuart was not exactly a secret, and yet I could feel my face burning red all the same. Red enough to match the ugly sweater my mom had bought me for the party, complete with shiny silver pom-poms that lit up. Stuart and I had been lab partners for the better part of the year, and I had broken no less than three glass beakers in that time, fumbling all over myself around him.

"Kiss him! Kiss him!"

Gemma jumped to her feet. "I think her blush confirms it, folks." She grabbed the mistletoe that was sloppily thumbtacked to a low basement ceiling beam and held it above my head.

"What do you think, Stuart?" Gemma waggled the mistletoe suggestively. "Want to lay one on her?"

"It's not my turn," he mumbled.

Did he not *want* to kiss me?

Was I that repulsive?

Could I die right here on the spot?

Another boy, Ryder, grabbed the mistletoe from Gemma and rubbed it sensually across his face. "Come on Holly, what do you see in him anyway? Why not me? Pucker up!"

"Ryder, don't be weird," said the girl next to him, grabbing the mistletoe and tucking it behind her ear like some kind of holiday elf. "Give the girl a break. She clearly doesn't want to play."

Yes, dying—right here—would be far superior to how the night was going.

"I have to go to the bathroom," I stammered, jumping to my feet and pushing Gemma out of the way. The other kids were laughing and tossing the mistletoe around between them, but I shoved my way through and toward the stairs to mask the fact that hot tears were threatening to spill from my face.

I closed the basement door behind me and sat on the lowest step, wiping at my eyes.

I shouldn't have come to the Christmas party.

Gemma and I had been friends since we were little, and I knew she meant well. But once we got to high school, she'd made a whole new group of friends. I guess that's what happens when you join cheerleading, ASB, and Key Club—to name a few of Gemma's new hobbies. Sure, her new friends tolerated me because they liked Gemma, but I'm not one of them.

I should have just let Gemma have her party. I—and Stuart, for that matter—didn't really belong here. We were nerds, and they were cool. It felt like such a high-school stereotype to admit, but it really was as simple as that. I let myself bask in self-pity another minute longer, then pushed myself up, determined to shake it off.

I didn't feel quite ready to go back into the basement though, so instead, I wandered up the carpeted stairs. Gemma's parents liked me. I certainly wasn't dressed for their party, but they probably wouldn't mind me popping in. Maybe it would give Gemma's friends time to move on to something else.

As I meandered up to the ground floor, I admired the strangeness of the Harpers' decor. No wonder they threw an annual no-holds-barred medieval yuletide celebration. That's just the kind of people they were. The staircase walls were adorned in medieval weaponry—swords, daggers, even an antique crossbow. They went to a lot of Renaissance festivals, and I think they even met doing some kind of LARP when they were younger. A wedding photo at the top of the stairs showed the two of them bedecked in ornate armor over their formal wear, their wedding party proudly holding swords above their heads.

Gemma was mostly embarrassed by it all, but I thought it was kind of cool.

Upstairs, old-timey music rife with fiddles and jingle bells filled the air, and adults in tightly laced bodices and elaborate hats mingled while eating delicate meats and cheeses with their bare hands. There was alcohol everywhere, which the Harpers' guests drank from all manner of bizarre receptacles, from glass goblets to giant pewter tankards to decorative drinking horns. Large tapestries were strung up on the walls, covering the Harpers' family photos, and antique candelabras dripped wax onto the hardwood table.

"Hey, Mr. and Mrs. Harper."

Gemma's parents stood beside a man dressed as a jester who was juggling fake snowballs while singing silly lyrics along to the music.

"Well met, Holly! How farest thou at the jolly youth party?" Mr. Harper asked with an exaggerated accent, cheeks rosy from the honey mead he was sipping.

I shrugged. "Oh, you know. It's Christmas-tastic."

"Not digging it?" He dropped the medieval bit. "Do I need to pop my head in?"

"I just need to use the bathroom," I insisted, trying to wave away the concern. A parental check-in was the last thing I needed. That would make me a wimp *and* a snitch. "Don't let me keep you from...." I gestured vaguely toward a group of women all stuffing mistletoe down their expansive cleavage, as if the activity spoke for itself.

"Methinks someone spiked the eggnog," Mr. Harper winked, then paused. "All good?" Mrs. Harper had already wandered away, and he seemed eager to join her.

"Have a good time." I darted to the bathroom as quickly as possible.

A few splashes of cold water to the face later, I finally took a long, deep breath.

I was ready to rejoin the downstairs party. Maybe. Probably.

Smoothing down my horrible sweater, I headed back toward the basement, but paused at the faint sound of a television left on in the den. Honestly, a bit of TV sounded more appealing than reentering that sweaty basement. Surely they wouldn't miss me for a while longer?

"Party-goers are advised to use caution this holiday season, as a particular strain of mistletoe seems to be having odd effects on those who interact with it."

I wondered if there was a special Christmas spoof on Saturday Night Live or something. Dangerous mistletoe? I love a good comedy sketch, so I turned up the volume, tucking my legs under me on the Harpers' overstuffed couch. Anything to avoid more "Spin the Bottle Truth or Dare."

But it wasn't SNL—it was a breaking story on the evening news. A shivering reporter stood in front of a hospital, wrapped in a puffy winter coat.

"The FDA is encouraging anyone with a live mistletoe plant to dispose of it immediately and to use hospital-grade gloves if possible as an added precaution. This story is still developing, but it appears those who come in direct contact with mistletoe are developing an unidentified illness."

They cut to a split screen, including a news anchor back in the station. *"Unidentified illness? What are the symptoms?"*

"We're getting reports that close human contact after direct exposure to this strain of mistletoe is causing people to act...strangely."

"Strange how?"

"It seems to be a kind of...aggression. It's really too early to say for sure, but the situation at various hospitals across the nation is getting serious. The best thing you can do now is get rid of the mistletoe and wait it out. We'll share more as we get the updates, folks, but for now, toss out that mistletoe." The reporter glanced over her shoulder then, as if making sure nobody infected with mistletoe was nearby.

"Is there...anything else they can do to protect themselves?" The news anchor looked quite relieved to be behind a desk, rather than out on location.

The reporter paused before answering. *"If you think you've been exposed to mistletoe, you should maintain a safe distance from others. That means no holiday smooching, folks, just to be safe. And please stay indoors, until we know more."*

"No smooching?" The anchor said in mock horror, trying her best to lighten the tone of the

broadcast. *"Well, this is certainly some terrible holiday news. Have we all been naughty this year?"*

"It sure does look that way. Stay safe out there, folks."

The news segment ended with a dramatic musical riff, and an extra-loud commercial for Ford trucks filled the screen.

For a moment, I wasn't sure what to do. There was mistletoe *everywhere* in the house.

I just had to gather it up. Throw it away.

I raced downstairs, heart pounding, and flung the door open.

"We have to get rid of the mistletoe!" I shouted without thinking, and the whole room fell silent. All heads turned to stare at me. I was out of breath.

Nobody reacted right away. They were still in a circle, clearly still playing. One boy—I think his name was Benji—had the mistletoe between his teeth.

"I'm serious," I said, louder this time. "Gather it all—and don't touch it anymore. We have to get it out of here."

Finally Gemma spoke, slowly and deliberately. "Holly. What's...going on?"

What wasn't she understanding about this? "We have to get rid of the mistletoe *right now*."

"Sorry, everyone..." Gemma addressed the room through gritted teeth. "Holly can be a little dramatic sometimes." Then she turned back to me. "Sidebar, over here?"

She pulled open a closet door, and two kids— Colby and Jules—tumbled out. "Sorry, we need the space," Gemma said, and Jules adjusted her skirt as Colby pulled her to her feet.

Gemma pushed me in and pulled the door shut behind us.

"Make out!" Ryder called from across the room.

"Die in a fire, Ryder!" Gemma shouted back.

"Classy friends," I muttered, and instantly regretted it—because Gemma turned on me.

"*Why* are you trying to ruin my party?" The light from the door slats shone on her face in harsh lines, making her look extra scary.

"I—what?"

"First you won't kiss Stuart—the whole reason I *invited* him—and now you're being so weird. If you don't want to play spin the bottle, just say so. But we aren't going to stop kissing just because you *get rid of the mistletoe*."

Only then did I realize what my warning probably looked like to the rest of them.

"It's not about *that*. It's about—the *mistletoe itself*—"

"What *about* the mistletoe?"

"*Listen* to me," I said, batting at a coat sleeve that was jutting into the side of my head. "I just saw a news broadcast. There's something wrong with it. They're saying not to kiss people near it."

"*OK*, Holly," Gemma said, clearly not believing a word I'm saying.

"I'm serious. It's real."

"This sounds like one of those things they tell kids to scare them into not touching each other. You know, like cooties, and mono."

"Mono is also real, Gemma."

"Okay, sure, but no one here *has* mono, no one has cooties, and no one has...mistletoe pox, or whatever you're talking about. Are you sure it wasn't my dad playing a prank? This sounds like a classic dad joke."

"No, I didn't hear this from your *dad*—"

"I'm going back to my party," she cut me off mid-sentence. "Are you coming with me?"

My heart was still hammering in my chest, but I hated when Gemma was mad at me. And the newscaster did say it was only *one* strain of mistletoe. What were the odds it was the same kind the Harpers decorated their house with?

"Okay," I relented. "I'm sorry."

"You all good?" Gemma asked, a bit more gently this time. She gave my arm a little squeeze.

Maybe she was right. It did sound pretty nonsensical, the more I thought about it. In fact, the longer I stood in the closet with Gemma, the more I second-guessed whether we needed to be concerned at all. The mistletoe was probably just making people itchy, like some kind of allergic reaction. What was the worst that could happen?

Gemma was my best friend, and she deserved a nice Christmas party—even if most of her new friends were annoying.

"I think I'm just on edge," I admitted, offering an olive branch, "since I don't know your friends very well."

"They're not as great as you, Holls, but they're fun. Come on."

We emerged from the closet, and Ryder let out a wolf whistle. "Seven minutes in heaven!" he whooped at us, and Gemma gave him a middle finger. Everyone looked exactly as we'd left them—bedecked in Christmas attire, rosy cheeked, and totally healthy.

I pushed the news broadcast from my mind and rejoined the circle.

"You're up, Ryder," Gemma grinned, rolling the champagne bottle in his direction. "Put your money where your mouth is. Or your mouth where…well, *just spin*."

It seemed my little outburst was forgotten, but I couldn't help but notice the sprig of mistletoe sticking out of the top of Ryder's pants.

Just enjoy the Christmas party, I told myself. And later, maybe try talking to Stuart alone.

Ryder gave a cocky flick of his hair, then twisted his wrist around to give the bottle a good spin. It whirled around and around, six, seven, eight, *nine* times, before starting to slow. Finally, the bottle came to a stop…a few inches past me, pointing directly at a girl I didn't know well named Whitney. I breathed a sigh of relief, making room for the two of them by scooting marginally closer to Stuart.

Ryder made a big show of spraying some kind of minty breath spray in his mouth, then leaned across the circle to kiss Whitney directly on the lips. He lost his balance and toppled over onto her, sending them both crashing back onto the carpet with a shared giggle. He kissed her more deeply then, pinning her to the ground while everyone watched.

Some of the others were cheering, and Fletcher let out a low whistle, but after a moment it appeared Whitney was no longer enjoying it.

In fact, it looked like she was struggling.

It seems to be a kind of…aggression.

My pulse quickened. "Whitney?"

Gemma shot me a look. I was being weird again—I knew it—but I couldn't get the newscasters out of my head.

No holiday smooching, folks.

"Hey, man, that's enough for one spin," Stuart said. "It's someone else's turn."

Ryder still hadn't let up, and Whitney was making a gagging sound now.

This was not normal.

"Somebody get him off her"—I rushed toward them, right as Whitney let out a blood-curdling scream.

The energy in the room changed instantly as the others finally realized something was really wrong. Fletcher and Colby jumped to attention, trying to grab onto either side of Ryder. Whitney was still screaming, and so was Mindy, who had a clear view of what was happening. Nobody could get him off of her.

I didn't think. I grabbed a vase off the side table near me and bashed it over Ryder's head. The shock of it knocked him out, and he collapsed, his weight continuing to pin Whitney down as pieces of porcelain cascaded down around them.

Nobody moved. Both Fletcher and Colby turned to me, eyes wide. Like *I* was the monster.

And yet, no one else seemed willing to *do* anything. I stepped forward and kicked Ryder over, his limp body rolling off of Whitney, who was crying and shuddering beneath him. There was a bloody gash along her cheek—he'd *bitten* her.

"Oh my god, Whitney!" Gemma cried, and the group's attention shifted—in horror—from me to her. Gemma pulled her friend to a sitting position, pulling her in for a hug before yelling, "Someone call an ambulance!"

I nodded, still disoriented by what Ryder had done—and what *I'd* done. Was *this* the mistletoe effect? Was this what the newscasters were talking about? I reached for my phone in my back pocket before remembering—no service in the basement. My phone was in my purse upstairs.

I pounded up the stairs, vision blurry, sweat pouring from beneath my hot sweater.

What was going *on?*

I darted past the medieval party, running back to the den where we'd stowed our purses and winter jackets. The TV was playing the late-night home-shopping network now, and I tuned it out, fumbling for my cell phone.

I punched in 911 as soon as I found it.

The line was… busy? Was that even possible?

I hung up and dialed again. Still busy.

I was starting to panic, but tried a third time. This time I got a frazzled-sounding voice on the other line. "Hello, this is 911. What is your emergency?"

"Hi, I'm at a party, and a boy just…bit someone? She's bleeding and needs help."

"Mistletoe?" the dispatcher asked, sounding tired.

I was so stunned I almost dropped the phone. "I'm sorry. What did you say?"

"Is there mistletoe there?"

Thud, thud, thud went my heart. "Um…well, it's a Christmas party. So yes."

"Are you a religious woman, ma'am?"

"Sorry?"

"If you are, I suggest praying. I've never seen anything like this before."

"*What*?"

"All ambulances are currently tied up. Get yourself to safety, if you can. We recommend arming yourself, or running, or both."

There was a pause, but I was too shocked to ask any follow-up questions.

"Merry Christmas," the voice said in a deadpan, and then the line went dead.

For a moment I stared at my cell phone, unable to believe I just got hung up on by 911.

What was wrong with the mistletoe? What had it done to Ryder?

Then it occurred to me — *Mr. and Mrs. Harper.*

Grown-ups! They could help. They would know what to do.

I stumbled into the kitchen, following the sounds of the music. A large group of grown-ups were huddled in the dining room, Mrs. Harper at the helm. I tapped urgently on her shoulder, not paying any mind to what they were actually doing. It was always some manner of ye olde weird activity, and that didn't matter right now.

"Mrs. Harper, something really strange is happening downstairs." My voice was tight and hurried as I struggled to get the words out without crying. "I think some of the kids are hurt, and —"

I stopped in my tracks.

Mrs. Harper turned slowly to look at me, blood rimming her lips. Her eyes were dark and wild, a look of frenzy behind her enlarged pupils. Not just Mrs. Harper — *all* the grown-ups looked weird. They shuffled behind her with an unnatural rigidity, their once-boisterous demeanors replaced with a chilling monstrousness.

Just like Ryder.

The light frivolity of my previous trip upstairs was gone — and in its place, a nightmare. Only then did I notice the blood pooling out from behind the dining room table.

I did not want to stick around to see what that had come from.

"Never mind." I backed up as quickly as I could, only knocking one chair over in my scramble to get away from them. My eyes drifted toward the back door, and I thought about what the 911 dispatcher had said.

Get yourself to safety.

It would be so easy to slip out into the night.

But then I thought of everyone trapped down in the basement with Ryder. They didn't know they were trapped, or that *this* was happening upstairs.

I had to warn them—to *save* them.

There was no time to lose. I threw myself into the stairwell leading down to the basement, slamming the door shut behind me before Mrs. Harper and the others could get any closer.

Stuart was waiting at the bottom, breathing heavily and leaning against the second door. I had almost forgotten about him in the shuffle. Earlier in the evening I might have relished the idea of finding him alone in the stairwell, but now all I could focus on were the shouts coming from inside.

"What's going on?"

"It's bad in there," he grimaced.

I frowned. "Upstairs, too."

Stuart's eyes widened. "Upstairs?"

I nodded grimly, and for a moment we stared at each other, as if not sure what to do next—knowing danger was waiting in either direction. I briefly wondered if he was also thinking about being alone in this dark stairwell with me, and how that might have been exciting given any other circumstances. But then I squashed my brief lapse in focus, pushing the thoughts from my mind. There were much more pressing matters to tend to presently, and besides, Stuart probably didn't think about me like that anyway.

"I have an idea." I thumped back up the stairs and began taking weapons off the wall. A set of daggers, a broadsword, the crossbow. Anything I could carry.

Stuart looked confused.

"Here." I thrust the sword at him. "We have to go back in."

Stuart gulped, but nodded and accepted the weapon.

Then I kicked the door open.

Gemma and Fletcher were fighting off a ravenous-looking Whitney with a floor lamp. Ryder was still passed out on the ground, and most of the other kids stood terrified in the corner.

"Here!" I tossed a dagger each to Gemma and Fletcher, keeping the crossbow for myself.

"Are you *crazy*?" Gemma asked, right as Whitney lunged for her. Gemma jumped on to the coffee table to avoid the attack, and Whitney missed her by mere inches, hurtling to the ground and taking the entire plate of chocolate chip cookies with her.

"What's *wrong* with them?" Fletcher looked panicked. He seemed more willing to use the dagger than Gemma, but was holding it all wrong. Unfortunately there was no time for a combat lesson.

"I don't know," I breathed, "but it's not just happening here. It's everywhere."

"But why?" Gemma asked from her spot on the table, her eyes full of tears as she stared aghast at the dagger in her hand. Whitney was on the cheerleading squad with her. Ryder was ASB president.

I gave her a look. "The *mistletoe*."

"What *about* the mistletoe?"

"I *told* you." I was getting tired of repeating it. "It's making people sick. It's making people...like that."

"I'm just going to say it," Fletcher said, still holding his dagger in a way that was more likely to hurt himself than anyone else. "They're zombies. The mistletoe turned them into zombies."

Gemma looked horrified. "Oh my god, Fletcher, you can't just say our friends turned into *zombies*."

But then Colby and Jules charged for her with the same odd, hungry look in their eyes that I saw in the adults upstairs. Their skin was pale and their fingers were curled unnaturally as they reached outward, more animalistic than human.

They sure looked like zombies to me.

Gemma yelped, reflexively slashing Colby in the face, but the dagger was so blunt it had no effect. "Holly, this is a glorified letter opener!" she screamed, tossing the dagger and resorting to kicking at Colby with the pointed toe of her sparkly party shoes. It knocked him back slightly, but Jules was still in hot pursuit.

I hoisted up my crossbow and pointed it at Colby, aimed, and pulled the trigger.

The bolt fired, hitting him square in the forehead...where it bounced comically to the floor.

The tip was made of foam. Foam arrows for a prop weapon.

So much for that idea.

Gemma saw me struggling and choked back a defeated sob as I tossed the crossbow to the side.

Fletcher had given up all pretense of fighting back and was cowering in the corner with the others, still clinging to the dagger I'd given him, but not using it—not that it would have helped anyway, with his form.

I tried to keep track of who had turned. Whitney. Ryder. Jules. Colby. Who else had touched the mistletoe? Who else had been kissing?

Everyone had played the game.

We needed to get out of here.

"*That's* not going to happen to us, is it?" Fletcher stammered. "I mean the rest of us?"

Everyone had passed the mistletoe around. Everyone had kissed someone else.

Except—

Stuart surged forward, using the edge of the broadsword like a shield as Jules came after me. It was enough to knock her down, enough to give me a moment to think.

I grabbed Gemma's hand, yanking her from the table and into the stairwell.

"If it *is* the mistletoe," I hissed at her, "then no one down here is safe. We need to go."

"But my friends" — she argued, trying to pull away — "and Fletcher — "

But just as the words left her mouth, two more people turned: Benji, Mindy. Then another three. I tried to remember their names as they changed, but it was happening so fast. Eric? Blair? Another blonde girl?

Fletcher was at the front of the pack, and for just a moment it looked as though he was going to try to do something heroic, maybe try to hold them back — but then his eyes went dark and glassy too, and he lumbered toward us.

I stopped trying to keep count. Within a moment it became clear that Gemma, Stuart, and I were the only ones left — with nothing to protect ourselves but a bunch of fake weapons.

I tried to stay calm. "Gemma, we need to leave."

The zombies backed Stuart into the doorway, where he did an admirable job fighting off the rabid party-goers by bludgeoning them with the prop sword.

Gemma's eyes widened, and she let out a little choking sob, standing there between us in her sequined dress and reindeer antlers.

"Gemma, *now.*"

But Gemma had collapsed to her knees, wracking sobs shaking through her. I thought about telling her what was going on upstairs as a way to get her to move, explaining what happened to her parents — but I couldn't bring myself to do it. She was already upset enough.

Stuart barely managed to keep the others at bay. "Holly. I can't close the door with her there."

"Give me thirty seconds," I said, then turned to Gemma, who was completely melting down.

"I just wanted to have a nice party," she said pitifully. "I just wanted people to *like* me."

"They *do* like you, Gemma," I said hurriedly. "A little too much right now, actually. So please stand up before your new friends eat us all."

But Gemma was beyond reasoning, tears falling in huge droplets down her cheeks as she stayed firmly planted in the doorway. I sighed, then hoisted her up by her armpits, dragging my hysterical friend across the carpet and out of the path of the door.

We were almost home free.

But then Gemma gave a small shudder, and her eyes went funny.

"Gemma, *no*." My voice was panicked. "Listen to me. You're okay. You're *okay*."

She stared back at me, and for a moment I saw her in there — my best friend since childhood, looking frightened and helpless in my arms.

"Gemma, *please*." The desperation in my voice was rising.

I was so focused on her that I didn't notice how much Stuart was struggling against the onslaught of zombies at the door. How he couldn't hold them all for much longer. Because if there was a chance that Gemma might be okay, then I had to save her. Maybe I just needed to get her away from everyone else. Maybe it would all be okay.

But then the moment passed. Her eyes clouded over; her lip curled back. In the blink of an eye, she was gone, her grip tightening on me until her fingernails broke through the skin on my arm.

"Holly, we need to go," Stuart said as calmly as he could. "She doesn't recognize you anymore."

I thought of the first time Gemma and I met — how we bonded over both choosing cherry popsicles from the neighborhood ice cream truck, giggling as the sticky juice dripped down our gangly little arms. Now it was my blood that smeared red against her porcelain skin, the innocence of our childhood erased in a single night.

"*Holly*!" This time Stuart shouted, and it was enough to snap me out of it. We'd never get the door shut behind us if we didn't move *now*. As if on cue, the Fletcher zombie broke through Stuart's barricade, the prop sword clattering to the ground as the group surged.

"Okay." My voice faltered as I saw what I had to do. "Okay." I pushed Gemma off of me, right into the oncoming Fletcher. Stuart and I used her as a sort of human battering ram, forcing all the zombies back into the basement. For a split second, I watched her stumble into the outstretched arms of her new friends. Yet again, I was not one of them.

And for the first time since we'd started high school, I was perfectly okay with that.

There was nothing I could do now, aside from slamming the door shut between us.

Stuart and I took only a moment to catch our breath before making our way up the stairs. This night was far from over. We emerged into the remains of the upstairs party, and I faintly wondered how much worse it could possibly be than the scene we'd just left behind.

The answer was a *lot* worse.

The grown-ups wandered around the ground floor feverishly, their elaborate costumes in bloody tatters like we were in some kind of whimsical haunted house. But there was no whimsy in their eyes as a few turned toward us. Only hunger.

"Um, I thought this spread through *kissing*." The color drained from Stuart's face at the sight of the upstairs party.

"I am not here to judge how grown-ups have fun." I paused, trying to remind myself that these were the Harpers' friends and not the next mob swarm in a video game. "Plus, there's mistletoe everywhere."

Just then the music changed from a jolly sea shanty to a much moodier Gregorian chant—a clear sign we had overstayed our welcome.

My heart pounded. "Got a plan?"

Stuart still looked a bit stunned. "I was hoping you did."

A woman dressed like Queen Elizabeth, complete with a high, feathered neckline and intricately beaded bodice, was leading the pack. Her skirts were ripped and caked in blood, one slipper-clad foot twisting distinctly the wrong way with each step.

"Back door is this way." I grabbed Stuart's hand, taking advantage of her limp to get away while we still could. "And best not be empty-handed." I swiped a ceramic reindeer from a Christmas display on our way toward the sliding glass door, which was open a crack.

Stuart didn't have time to grab anything of his own before the crowd started closing in on us. We were faster than most of the zombies, but a large man in a Viking costume plowed over Queen Elizabeth in hot pursuit. I managed to slip through the opening in the sliding glass door, but Stuart wasn't so lucky. The Viking edged him out of the way with a hard shoulder check, focused only on me and the open doorway.

"Holly—watch out!" Stuart was knocked backward as the Viking threw the sliding door open with a bang.

The Viking hurled himself in my direction, hands outstretched and clawing at my puffy sweater. Behind him, Stuart was attempting to hold back yet another doorway of oncoming zombies, and all I had to protect myself with was a stolen dollar-store reindeer. It felt comically ineffective as I swung repeatedly at his chest.

Stuart edged through the door, slamming it shut and wedging a nearby lawn chair against the handle to keep the other zombies at bay. Then he jumped and grabbed a string of Christmas lights hanging from the eaves of the house.

The lights flickered and blinked out, washing the yard in darkness.

"This is no time for redecorating!" I yelped. Stuart ran toward the Viking — letting loose some kind of battle cry — and wrapped the lights tightly around his body: two, three, four times. His beefy arms were pinned decoratively to his sides, and for a moment, our Viking friend looked just disoriented enough to give me a burst of courage.

I took my shot, kicking a leg under the Viking and knocking him to the ground, where he struggled against his festive bindings.

Stuart looked impressed. "Wow. Nice job."

My hands were shaking, and sweat dripped down the back of my neck. "You did most of it." I shrugged off his compliment.

"Sure, if 'most of it' was teeing him up for your complete and utter badassery."

I blushed, despite myself. "Well, thanks. We should be safe for a while now."

Not a moment after the words had left my mouth, the back door *exploded*. Medieval zombies spilled from the wreckage as glass shards littered the ground around them. It was a veritable sea of brocade and lace and feathers, led by a man with a blood-stained ruffle around his neck who I recognized to be Gemma's uncle. Usually he told the worst puns, but tonight, there were no bad jokes to be heard. Only the terrifying moans of dozens of deranged, costumed zombies.

"No," Stuart said, looking frantically around for more Christmas lights. "*No!*"

"There's too many of them." I felt my stomach drop. "We can't fight them all."

Stuart hopped from foot to foot with nervous energy, trying to come up with a plan. I followed his gaze as he sized up the wooden fence.

"Think we can make it?"

I shrugged my shoulders. We were quickly running out of time. "Only one way to find out."

There was a foothold partway up; Stuart gave me a boost. I managed to pull myself up, balancing on the top of the fence for a moment as Stuart threw a leg over as well. The swarm was getting closer. I watched as a woman in a frock lunged at him before he could hook his other leg over the top of the fence.

"Look out!" I jumped down to the other side. The frock zombie had hold of his sleeve, which he quickly shimmied out of, letting her take the entire green flannel in exchange for hurtling himself over the fence while she was distracted. He landed with a thud beside me.

For a moment we crouched in the grass, breathing heavily, listening to the frantic scrabbling on the other side of the fence.

Once we caught our breath, a terrible thought occurred to me. I gave Stuart a sidelong glance. "My parents dropped me off," I said miserably. "Did you drive?"

For the first time since people started turning into zombies, Stuart flashed me the grin that gave my stomach butterflies in chemistry class. "My car is parked just down the street."

"I could kiss you," I said without thinking.

Stuart looked horrified.

"Hypothetically!" I corrected myself, jumping to my feet. I wasn't sure if he looked so alarmed because of the present situation or because the idea of kissing me was so terrible, but I didn't have time to unpack our current relationship status. Our lives were at stake.

We ran into the front yard together, Stuart already digging his keys from his pocket. They jingled in his hand — a sound of freedom and hope. But when we got to the driveway, we stopped dead in our tracks.

The street ahead was *filled* with meandering zombies: a mishmash of people in cocktail dresses and ugly sweaters, and one guy lumbering around in a full-on Santa Claus suit.

Stuart's jaw dropped. "How many Christmas parties *were* there tonight?"

There was no way we'd make it to his car in one piece. Not right now, at least.

"Okay, new plan." I turned and led us back toward Gemma's house. "See that trellis?" I pointed to a wooden structure covered in knotted wisteria that framed the picture window. "Gemma and I used to climb it as kids."

"Higher ground," Stuart nodded. "Smart."

Some of the mistletoe zombies in the street had started to notice us. I quickened my pace. "Hope you're not afraid of heights."

"You know," he reasoned, "I'm *more* afraid of zombies."

"Great!" I reached up and grabbed onto the trellis, hoping it could handle my weight as well as it did when I was eleven. It seemed to sag a bit under the pressure of my tennis shoes, but once I was confident it wouldn't buckle, I scrambled my way up one foothold at a time. Stuart was hot on my heels as the Santa zombie shambled toward us—but we were too fast for him. Stuart managed to pull himself up over the edge of the roof before the zombie even got within scratching distance.

Santa couldn't climb. Instead, he paced the grass below us, waiting, his snarls in stark contrast with the cheery jingling coming from his boots.

We rolled onto our sides and stayed there a moment, catching our breaths, not daring to move. The cacophony of guttural zombie noises echoed through the cool winter air, and we slowly, silently inched ourselves a bit higher up on the roof, just in case.

I'm not sure how long we laid side by side in silence, listening to the terrifying sounds below. Finally, when my heartbeat had returned to what felt like a semi-normal cadence, I broke the silence. "I think we'll be okay up here until morning."

Stuart began to shiver as a snowflake came to rest on his bare arm.

"If we don't die of hypothermia." He gritted his teeth.

For the first time all night, I was thankful for my dorky pompoms. "This is a pretty warm sweater." I paused. "We could...huddle for warmth."

He nodded, scooting a bit closer. His arm pressed up against mine.

Just huddling for warmth. It's a necessity. Don't read into it, Holly.

I stayed quiet for a moment, trying to block out the horrors of the evening. It was difficult, to be honest, what with our excellent view of the hordes of zombies overrunning the neighborhood down below.

"I'm so sorry," I said finally.

"For what?"

Stuart's teeth were chattering, and I risked scooting just a bit closer.

"It's my fault you're here," I said. "Gemma only invited you because...." I trailed off, realizing what I almost just admitted.

Stuart gave me a side glance. "Because?"

I took a deep breath. No time like the zombie apocalypse to just rip off the Band-Aid and come clean to your crush. "She invited you because she thought she could get us together."

Stuart caught a little flake of snow on his tongue. "Okay, I wouldn't call almost murdering everyone we know a *great* first date, but...it kind of worked."

My head shot in his direction. "What worked?"

"Well, look at us. The survivors. Having this romantic moment in the snow, before Christmas, while we hide from zombies."

I rolled my eyes. "Sure, but we're the survivors because we're the only losers who didn't kiss each other during that stupid game."

Stuart gave me a funny little grin. Then he pushed a piece of hair back from my face, which was slick with someone else's blood.

"Holly, not kissing you tonight was the best decision I ever made."

"Wow, I'm touched," I said flatly.

"I bet kissing isn't even all it's cracked up to be."

This surprised me. "You've never kissed anyone?"

He shrugged. "After tonight, I'm not sure I ever will."

My heart was still pounding — though from the horde of zombies below or my proximity to Stuart, I wasn't sure.

"Well," I reasoned, working up the courage to say something bold, "if we ever recover from the trauma of what happened at this party...I'd like to try and change your mind."

Stuart smiled, then took my arm and placed it around his shoulder, snuggling into my side. "I'd like that." He leaned his head against my shoulder, a red pompom pressing against his cheek.

"To years of therapy?" I asked.

Stuart laughed. "To years of therapy."

And there we sat: safe, together — watching the snow come down around us, the sounds of zombie wails and emergency sirens echoing off into the distance.

Not a sprig of mistletoe in sight.

Cultivate

by Katrina Hamilton

August knocked loudly on the wooden door of the old hovel, his frozen fingers attempting to overcome the sound of the howling wind. His boots were wet and beginning to freeze solid. It had been foolish to press on after dark with the snow still falling, but he wanted desperately to make it to Middlebury and sleep in a proper bed at an inn. Instead, he was going to be stuck yet again with whatever pitiful pile of straw and linens the country locals could provide.

He knocked again, loud and insistent. Someone must be home; he could see light in the foggy windows. The shack was built halfway into the hillside, both a building and a cave. Hopefully that meant it could keep the heat from a fire well.

August examined the front of the hovel again. There were no names nor markings of any kind, but hanging above the door was a bouquet of greens with plump white berries bunched up against the stems — a small sign of growth in the dark of winter.

The door creaked open slightly, and August caught a glimpse of a woman's face. "It's an odd hour for visitors," said the woman, her voice low and steady.

"I beg your pardon, madam," said August. "I was traveling through and got caught in the storm. I was hoping you and your husband might have an open bed for a stranger."

"Haven't got a husband," she said. "Nor a bed."

"Even a warm spot by the fire would be better than out here," he said, trying to walk the line between respectful and pitiful. "Please, ma'am. Just a spot to dry my boots and warm my heart."

"Your heart?" said the woman. She sized him up. "I don't suppose I could turn down such a request as that. Not in this weather anyway." She smiled and opened the door to welcome him in.

Inside, August shook the snow from his coat and began to pull off his traveling clothes.

"There's a chair over by the fire," said the woman. "You can leave it all to dry over there."

The room was lit bright with candles and a roaring fire in the corner. August could see the woman more clearly now, though he still had difficulty placing her. She was too old to be a maiden, but too young to be a hag. A few strands of gray seemed to shimmer against her brown hair in the firelight. Her dress and apron seemed well-worn, like any country woman, but the fabrics were too expensive for farm clothes. August hadn't seen wool so smooth or silk so fine outside of the universities, and even then, it was only on his wealthier classmates and colleagues. He'd always resented it on them, but on this middle-aged country woman, it intrigued him.

"You live alone, then?" he asked, placing his coat on the wooden chair by the fire.

"I do," she said. Her back was to him as she shuffled together some papers on a desk in the corner. There was no bed in this main room, but it seemed to otherwise contain every function of the house: the fire, the kitchen cupboards, a writing desk, and even a large and beautiful armchair, which felt out of place in the rustic setting. All around him were letter boxes and books stacked on top of each other, as well as herbs growing in small jars.

"I've not known many women who lived alone," August said, doing his best to fill the silence. "You're not scared at all, being by yourself like this?"

The woman turned, a slight smile on her face. "Scared?" she said. "Of whom should I be scared?"

"Well," August said, "not every man who raps on your door is going to be an upstanding citizen."

"And that's what you are, I assume? An upstanding citizen?"

"Of course," he said. "I'm a scholar by trade. I'm hoping to find a teaching position in Middlebury." August sat in the chair to unlace his boots. "If I ever get there, of course. The man in Providence said it was only two days' walk, and I've already gone three."

"Then perhaps I'm not the one who needs protection from unscrupulous men," she said. "It's another two days to Middlebury from here, even in good weather."

"Damn," said August under his breath. He looked up at her, catching himself. "Begging your pardon, ma'am."

"I've heard worse words from better men," she said. She held a cup to her lips and took a slow sip. "But to your earlier question," she said, taking a seat in the large armchair. "You needn't worry about me. It's the time of the great winter feasts, and I have protection." She gestured above the door. On the inside frame was another bundle of that same white-berried green.

"What is it?" he asked.

"Mistletoe," she said. "The Romans saw it as a sign of peace and protection. They hung it in their doorways during the Saturnalia."

"Few common people know the traditions of the great Roman civilization," he said. "Are you educated?"

"Quite well," she replied, before quickly returning to the subject. "It's also good for keeping out demons and witches."

"Do the people out here in the country still believe in witches?" he asked, a small laugh on his lips.

"Only those that haven't seen them," she replied.

It was a puzzling phrase, but August didn't want to appear too stupid for her joke. He nodded and smiled back. "It's funny," he said. "After all those great traditions, all I ever heard about mistletoe back in boarding school was that if you caught a girl under it, she was compelled to kiss you."

"That seems to me a dreadfully poor deal for the girls," she said.

"Only for those who didn't want it," he said. "For others, it was a good way to gain a kiss but maintain your virtue."

"You encountered a lot of girls of that nature, I assume?"

"More than their kin would care to admit," he said. It was too bold a thing to say to a stranger, especially a woman, but she seemed so calm that August felt like he could say almost anything to her.

"Perhaps they were raised in less-than-virtuous households," the woman said.

"Some were," said August. "And some just needed...convincing." Again, too bold.

"Convincing?"

"Please don't mistake me for some sort of scoundrel," he said. "But young boys are...of a sort. You understand."

"I understand." She took another sip from her mug, but kept her eyes on him. August looked around the room, doing his best to gain a few more clues to this stranger's station: A grown woman, unmarried, educated, but living alone in the woods and wearing old but fine clothes. Perhaps she was a wealthy heiress in hiding.

"You said you were hoping for a teaching position?" she asked.

"Yes," he said. "I had one in Providence, but...I felt as though I'd outgrown it."

"So you haven't an offer in hand for Middlebury?"

"No," he said, doing what he knew to be a poor job of hiding his embarrassment. "I wrote letters ahead, but I've yet to hear back. However, my experience in the city should more than qualify me for any position out there. I decided to make the journey early in anticipation of employment."

"And what does your family think of such bold action?" she asked.

"My mother passed away when I was a child," he said, "and I haven't spoken to my father in some time. Until I find a wife, I'm afraid I haven't much family to speak of."

"Many would call that a pity," she said.

"Many would," he replied.

Her eyes narrowed, and he caught her smiling again. "How inconsiderate of me," she said abruptly. "You are frozen solid, and I haven't offered you any tea."

"Tea would be greatly appreciated," he said. "Thank you."

The woman got up, her long skirt trailing behind her as she walked over to the wash table to fill a kettle with water. Above the table, August spotted a vine from one of the jars creeping across the length of the ceiling, and he wondered how long she'd lived in this place. The woman set the pot to boil over the fire, then returned to her chair.

"I'm sure you've gathered by now that I tend to keep to myself," she said. "Still, it is nice to have a man of learning in the house."

"I'm honored," he said. "I have to say, I feel quite at ease around you."

"Is that so?" she asked.

"Yes," he said. "I suppose it's not often that I am in the company of women under such...casual circumstances." He gestured down to his stocking feet.

"Of course," she said. "You're used to all those unvirtuous schoolgirls."

August laughed. "I outgrew the schoolgirls long ago. Unfortunately, I don't understand the courtship of adult women at all. It seems even more...contradictory."

"It is the curse of man," she said.

"To court women?"

"To be confounded by them."

Bubbling noises were coming out of the kettle, and the woman got up to retrieve the hot water. She brought it over to the cupboards and began to prepare the tea.

"I much prefer the mating and settlement habits of plants," she said over her shoulder, her back to him.

"I noticed you have an affinity," he said. The more he looked for them, the more plants seemed to appear in every corner of the room. "Have you made a study of horticulture?"

"Something like that," she said. "For example, the mistletoe there. It is quite beautiful and useful. Doctors of old Europe used it to treat pain in the bones, as well as fits of seizure. Not to mention women have used it for centuries to...rid themselves of undesired troubles."

"Troubles?"

"The kind of troubles that convincing men put into your belly."

August cleared his throat and swallowed. Now she was the one speaking out of turn. He'd never imagined someone discussing such things so openly, especially a woman to a man. She turned back to him, steaming cup in hand, and gently walked over to hand it to him.

"Thank you," he said. He blew lightly over the top of the cup to cool it before taking an impatient sip. "It's quite good. Thank you."

"It is my pleasure." Her smile was kind, almost maternal. She took a long drink from her own cup. There was silence between them. Any last remnant of tension slipped away as they each sipped their tea and listened to the howling wind and dull drip of snow on the roof.

"It's a parasite. Did you know that?" she said, finally breaking the silence.

"Excuse me?" said August.

"The mistletoe. It's a parasite. It grows on the branches of other trees, pulling life from them."

"Fascinating," he said. "And does it kill the tree?"

"It can," she said. "If it's allowed to grow strong enough."

"It seems terribly dangerous to keep such a species around," he said. "It could start killing the neighboring forest."

"A common concern," she said, "but there are layers to death. Sometimes the mistletoe will overtake the leaves of a tree but keep the trunk, feeding back as much as it draws away. A new essence in an old shell."

"Still," he said, "for the safety of the surrounding plant life, it seems better to kill a parasite rather than help it."

"The world needs parasites," she said.

This statement surprised August, and he looked up at the woman to see if she was serious. But as he tried to focus on her face, his vision began to blur. He felt a nausea creeping across his stomach.

"The natural order must be disrupted periodically," she continued, "or systems of growth will run too quickly to their inevitable ends."

August's heart began to beat stronger, and he felt as though the blood was draining from his head. He looked down at the cup in his hands and realized too late that he never saw her pour the tea into her own cup.

"Without the interruption of parasites, the strong will overtake the weak," said the woman. "The homogeny will destroy the diverse." She stood up, calmly setting her cup down as August's cup fell from his hands and he collapsed onto the floor. "Don't worry," she said, staring down at him. "It will make sense to you soon."

"What...what have you..." August was fighting for his words. He saw a flash of green light across her eyes. "You're a witch..."

The woman scoffed. "Witches are human," she said. "But people have been known to call me that. They'll call you the same."

"Me?" His voice was weak and unsteady.

"You should consider yourself fortunate," she said. "We normally devour men and only spread to women. But I think you'll like your new life as one of us." She leaned down over his convulsing body. "I think it will suit you. There will be no need to feign gratitude or reciprocate the goodwill of others."

The woman placed her hand on August's chest, and he watched as thin, green tendrils grew from her fingertips and began to pierce his skin, driving straight into his heart.

"You will find it much less...contradictory."

Rewind

by Sunny Everson

The Blockbuster on Market Street was the only place left in town to rent movies. Corporate had seen to that. The Safeway used to have video rentals up front, but when a new manager took over, the rental section had been shut down swiftly and without explanation. Carl at the Quik Stop had offered VHS rentals for a while, but word had somehow gotten around that his rentals were for a very specific adult demand, and Carl had shut it down when some of the Catholic families started boycotting his store.

Which left Blockbuster. The temple of fluorescent lights and over-priced candy. The church of yellow and blue. The mecca of commercial Hollywood.

For Frankie, working at the corporate video store was like working at a library that only shelved a dozen Nancy Drew knockoffs and charged you half the cover price just to borrow the books. But it paid a dollar an hour better than the overnight dishwasher position down at Greta's 24/7 Diner, which was what he'd been doing before.

The customers were about 50 percent regulars who came in once or twice a week for their movie nights and 50 percent random folks looking for something to watch for date night. It got a little slower in the fall when the kids first went back to school, but slowly ramped back up as the weather turned frigid and there was nothing left to do but sit at home and stare at the TV.

Christmas break had just started, and parents all around town were already looking for an electronic babysitter for a few hours.

A new crate of VHS tapes was waiting for Frankie when he came in for his Thursday closing shift. Out front, his coworker Kyle was neck-deep in a monologue with one of the regulars, Mrs. Miller, about the use of live penguins in *Batman Returns* while her four children shrieked and poured their allowances into the gumball machines, one quarter at a time. Frankie's personal policy was to avoid talking to customers unless it was absolutely necessary. He busied himself with the new crate.

There were half a dozen extra copies of each of the biggest hits of the year (*Lethal Weapon 3*, *Wayne's World*, *Sister Act*, etc.), but it was mostly summer blockbusters that had failed to garner much attention in theaters. He carried the crate around the store, arranging the films slowly on end caps in their various genre sections.

At the bottom of the crate, though, was a single copy of a direct-to-video Christmas movie. He left the crate in the back and carried the tape out to the section where the holiday videos lived, near the front of the store.

It was strange to get a new Christmas film so late. Most of them had come in right before Thanksgiving, because people inevitably got pumped for the next holiday before the current one was even over yet.

The movie was called *The Mistletoe Paradox*.

Frankie turned it over to read the synopsis.

After unexpectedly winning the lotto, Julie returns to her quaint hometown to throw a bridal shower for her sister. When she meets Keith, the handsome concierge at her festive hotel, sparks fly as she must help him save the beautiful hotel from being torn down! A new Christmas classic for all generations!

It sounded exactly like half the holiday movies Blockbuster already had on the shelves. It looked like it, too: the front cover was a woman with shoulder-length, brown hair in a red sweater with snow-covered trees and a brooding man in a nondescript, black button-up lurking in the background. Frankie squished it onto the shelf next to over a dozen other movies with nearly identical covers — then rearranged it three times for good measure, until Mrs. Miller and her brood left the store.

There were only five days left before Christmas, and he honestly didn't expect it to get much attention in that time. Seemed like a waste for corporate to have mailed it to them so late. They would have gotten more success out of a badly animated children's movie about a dog or a reindeer or something.

He was surprised later when Reuben Sterling came up to the register with it in his hand. He was a big man who always wore flannels and worked as a contractor rebuilding roofs and porches. He scowled when Frankie raised an eyebrow at his movie choice.

"The missus wants a Christmas movie," he grumbled, handing over a few bills to pay.

"Well, good luck," Frankie replied. "Doubt the acting's anything fantastic."

"Hmm," Reuben said. "Uh-huh. The acting."

"If you're looking for good acting," Kyle said from where he was spraying Windex on the front door, "you should definitely see *Bugsy*."

Reuben didn't acknowledge him on his way out.

———

Frankie worked a mid-shift the next day, which required him to wake up before noon and stagger into the store still bitterly half asleep.

He was glowering down at the register when the bell on the door rang and a customer came in. They set a movie down on the counter to return it.

"Thanks," Frankie started to grumble automatically—and turned to see it was Reuben. The scowl was gone from the contractor's face. He stood up straight, a smile on his face and a cliché twinkle in his eyes. "Good movie, then?" Frankie asked, a bit startled. He'd never seen Reuben smile before.

"We didn't actually watch it," Reuben said, chuckling. "After I left here last night, I went to check my lotto tickets. We won!" He blurted with a grin. "It was only a few hundred, but" —Reuben bellowed a louder laugh—"better than a damned movie, eh?"

Frankie tried to muster up a feeling of excitement for the man's luck, but to be honest, Reuben had already been making significantly more money as a contractor than Frankie ever would as a video rental cashier. "That's funny," he ended up saying. "Just like in the movie."

Reuben blinked confused at him, so Frankie held *The Mistletoe Paradox*'s cover up. "She wins the lotto at the beginning, it says."

The contractor chuckled. "Yeah, sure, just like the movie." He patted him on the shoulder more affectionately than Frankie thought was warranted for their cashier-and-customer relationship, slapped two dollar bills on the counter with a wink, and started for the door. "Happy holidays, my friend!" The doorbell rang again as he left.

"Wow, good for him!" Kyle exclaimed from somewhere nearby. Of course he had been listening.

Frankie turned back to the bulky gray computer on the counter. He checked the movie back in and slowly returned it to its spot with the more mature Christmas films, one shelf over from *The Muppet Christmas Carol* and the Mary Kate and Ashley Christmas special, *To Grandmother's House We Go*. That was the last he expected to see of the tape honestly, because with so many other generic, cookie-cutter holiday movies to pick from, what were the chances someone else would pick that one?

Less than two hours later, Frankie was looking down at the same movie cover when it was slapped down on the counter in front of him.

This time the customer was a middle-aged woman with bleached-blond hair and a white winter jacket on—Kathleen Bronson, who owned the salon two streets over. He imagined she had a bottle of wine in the car to drink while she watched it. She was that sort of person.

"Sounds real exciting, eh?" he asked her as he scanned the barcode into the computer.

She shrugged, adding a box of Butterfinger BB's to the counter. "There were two with car crashes in them, but the love interest looks cuter in this one."

Frankie paused. He didn't remember a car crash being mentioned in the movie description when he'd read it the day before. He turned the case over and scanned the synopsis again.

After a terrible car accident kills her fiancé, Julie returns to her quaint hometown to reconnect with her family. When she meets Keith, the man who was saved when he received her fiancé's heart, sparks fly as she must help him save the town from an ancient holiday curse! A new Christmas classic for all generations!

Frankie frowned. He reread the title again. "*The Mistletoe Paradox,*" it still said.

"Huh," he said, sliding the movie back across the counter to her.

"Yeah, sounds real thrilling," the woman said, perplexed by his confusion. "Well, thanks." She pulled it from his grasp and left.

He must have read the back of a different movie the day before. But hadn't he just talked to Reuben about it? Frankie shook his head. There must have been two movies with the same title with pretty much the same cover. All of those holiday movies were interchangeable anyway.

He was turning away to reshelve some misplaced titles when there was a screech of tires and loud crash outside. Frankie whirled back around to look out the front windows.

Kathleen hadn't checked while pulling out of the parking lot and had slammed her Buick into a passing sedan.

Frankie was using the phone at the register to report the accident to the cops when he realized.

"Please state the nature of your emergency," the operator's monotone voice said in his ear, but Frankie was staring out the window at the crashed cars, his mouth hanging open.

The movie.

The day before, the synopsis had mentioned the fictional protagonist Julie winning the lotto, and Reuben's lotto tickets had won that same day. And now the synopsis mentioned Julie getting in a car crash, and Kathleen had almost immediately crashed her car.

(Outside, Kathleen and the other driver had climbed from their cars, seemingly unscathed, and were engaged in a screaming match in the middle of the street.)

"Is anyone there? Are you hurt?" the emergency operator asked on the other end.

Frankie shook himself out of it. "Uh, no, sorry. I'm not hurt. There's been an accident on Market Street outside of the Blockbuster. Probably no injuries."

He hung up before the operator could ask more questions.

Waking up earlier than usual was making him paranoid. There was no reason to believe the VHS cassette had any effect on what happened to the people who checked it out. After all, Reuben had bought those lotto tickets days before renting the movie out. And Kathleen was probably a bad driver all the time. She just happened to get in a crash right outside the store. It was purely coincidental.

Still, when a cop returned the movie to the store the next day after fishing it out of Kathleen's totaled car, Frankie eyed it suspiciously.

"Weirdly diligent cop," Kyle said behind him after the officer left, and Frankie nodded along, trying to act normal.

When Kyle had walked away, he double-checked the back. The synopsis still talked about Julie's fiancé dying in a car crash. He must have been right before.... Reuben had checked out a different but eerily similar movie than Kathleen had gotten.

There wasn't anything strange about the tape except that someone had spent money making a movie that had already been made a dozen times with pretty much the same plot. No Christmas miracles here.

———

The next afternoon, Frankie got stuck on register again while Kyle took the deposit to the bank. A younger lady (he recognized her from the public library, but couldn't remember her name) brought *The Mistletoe Paradox* up to the counter to check out.

"My sister's kids are all adopted," she said without being prompted. "I go nuts for corny stuff like this."

Frankie tried not to gasp as he flipped the case over with a clatter, leaning down to read the synopsis on the back.

After Julie's boyfriend proposes, she returns to her quaint hometown to tell her family and begin planning the wedding. When she meets Keith, an exotic dancer with a big secret, sparks fly as she must help him find foster homes for homeless kids for the holidays! A new Christmas classic for all generations!

"No shit," Frankie swore out loud.

"Is something wrong?" the woman asked, doe eyes wide with alarm.

He didn't know how to explain without sounding completely off his rocker, so Frankie just coughed and scanned the barcode. "Do you have a boyfriend?" he asked as he slid the case back across the counter to her.

Her doe eyes got even wider. "Uh, yes, I do. Sorry. I'm sure you're really great, though," she stammered.

Frankie managed to not roll his eyes at her. "I'm sure he'll love the movie."

She nodded and left, looking both a little confused and a little nervous.

The next day (Christmas Eve, another mid-shift), she returned the movie with a very shiny new ring on her left hand and a glowing smile.

———

Now that the holiday had actually begun, the traffic slowed significantly, giving Kyle an unwarranted opportunity to share his cinematic knowledge aloud.

"Did you hear about the new Bill Murray film? It's called *Groundhog Day*."

Frankie went about dusting all of the shelves, trying not to watch Kyle reshelve *The Mistletoe Paradox*. He meticulously wiped down the corners of each shelf, pulling up years of dust.

"I was reading this interview in *Film Comment* with Harold Ramis, who directed and helped write it…."

What if he took the movie home? Would he suddenly inherit money or lose his job and have to move back in with his parents? Or perhaps he would break something important or find out his grandma had died? Would he meet the love of his life and learn the true meaning of Christmas?

Frankie found himself stopping, unable to begin dusting the final shelf: the holiday movies.

"If you remember," Kyle was still droning on, "Ramis and Murray worked together on both *Caddyshack* and *Ghostbusters*."

He moved his eyes slowly past animated *Frosty the Snowman* and James Stewart in *It's a Wonderful Life*. The woman in the red sweater on the cover of *The Mistletoe Paradox* seemed to be making direct eye contact with him.

He glanced around. The store was empty except for Kyle, who had lost track of *Groundhog Day* in favor of a wormhole of *Ghostbusters* trivia.

Frankie snatched the cover off the shelf and turned it around. What kind of mysterious incident would befall him if he checked it out? He held his breath as he read....

After a terrible accident leaves Julie with amnesia —

"Nope!" Frankie said, louder than he meant to.

"What's that?" Kyle asked, looking over.

But Frankie was already going to the front door, pausing with his hand hovering over the handle. He wanted to chuck the VHS as far as he could across the parking lot, but what if opening the door with it was what caused it to happen? Was it picking it up or checking it out? If he set it back down now, would he be free of its curse?

There was only one way to find out.

Frankie pivoted away from the door, forcing a smile onto his face. "Hey Kyle," he said "have you seen this one yet?"

Trusty Milo™'s Original Merry Mistletoe Moonshine for Authentic Holiday Cheer

by Jennifer Lee Swagert

Looking for the perfect blend of nutrition and cheer for your holiday interval celebration? Look no further than this safe and nourishing Trusty Milo™ recipe!

There's a reason Trusty Milo™ Moonshine is a staple good in every contractor's home. I've been drinking Trusty Milo™ Moonshine every holiday interval as far back as I can remember! Ever since entering adulthood, I've worked toward one goal: earning enough credits for my very own intervals. Guess what? This nutri-girl did it!

The day my boss granted me annual intervals, I cried tears of pure joy. Sure, I'd miss working, but my aches and sores would benefit from rest. Rest isn't enough, though. We all know that. We need nourishment, and there's only one trusted source that has our backs when it comes to nourishment packages! That's why I knew right away what I wanted my holiday interval to look like: a few hours in the media center with some Trusty Milo™ Moonshine.

For those who don't know, Moonshine is a traditional, liquid-based meal from Earth. Even people on Earth valued liquid nourishment (so don't go believing BOG's bogus claims to the contrary)! These meals are traditionally mixed at home and focus on funky flavors. In honor of tradition, Trusty Milo™ has released a new holiday delight: Authentic Mistletoe Prong.

"Extremely Safe & Delicious!"

Mistletoe is a rare plant on Earth with a fleshy prong and green color. It was traditionally consumed during holiday celebration meals on Earth. That's right: Trusty Milo™ made it possible for all of us to have access to a rare and precious plant this holiday interval! Each Trusty Milo™Mistletoe Package is thoroughly tested during development to ensure optimal nutrient density and safety.

Despite this dedication to our nutrition, Trusty Milo™still finds itself the target of intrusive scrutiny. Yes, BOG still requires everyone, including simple contractors like me, to add the usual obnoxious warning (despite no corroboration from Trusty Milo™):

Bureau of Government Health Authority Warning
1. Moonshine is not BOG-approved
2. Consumption of Moonshine beverages is hazardous to your health
   a. Minor symptoms include fever, chills, nausea, fatigue

    b. Major symptoms include cancer and death
3. Consumption of Moonshine beverages impairs neurological processes
4. Out of people who consume Moonshine, 68% of people will become seriously ill and 12% of people will die

---

Trusty Milo™ clarifies that this warning is based on bogus information and a distortion of the truth. Volunteers who participated in BOG-controlled studies self-reported their physical wellness, which means the data is fallible. Responses can be faked by elites in the research industry or by the participants themselves. We have no way of knowing whether or not the participants were paid to provide specific responses.

Save up your credits and buy some Authentic Mistletoe Prong at your local depot. Yep, they made it available in all public markets. As always, they stick to that trusty refrain: Nourish Everyone!

If you're worried about the mean-spirited investigations into unsafe ingredients in these products, don't be. If you ask me, these accusations against Trusty Milo™ are fabrications designed to restrict your access to nourishment and funky flavors. Many of us have been enjoying Trusty Milo™'s Nourish Line products our entire lives, and it's thanks to these nutrient-dense products that we've been able to stay upright and pain-free at work, especially during those 32-hour shifts! I'm personally grateful I've been able to stay nourished. Trusty Milo™ products enabled me to work hard and earn that interval. Take it from those of us who grew up enjoying their products our whole lives: you're safe.

For those of us whose parents worked hard enough to afford us Moonshine during holiday intervals, let me tell you: it was worth the credits! We spent our intervals nourished, safe, and full of cheer. I know I wasn't the only one worried our childhood memories would be taken away when BOG threatened action against Trusty Milo™! With the release of this fresh, unique product, it looks like Trusty Milo™ is here to stay.

If you're anything like me, the holiday interval can't come soon enough! For those of you who have yet to earn your holiday intervals, remember: These kinds of rewards are just around the corner! Stay on that line!

Happy Interval! May everyone be nourished!

Trusty Milo™'s Original Merry Mistletoe Moonshine for Authentic Holiday Cheer

Trusty Milo™ Authentic Mistletoe Prong brings a fresh, Earth flavor to a holiday interval classic! Best served in genuine glassware.

Prep Time	Cook Time
15 minutes	24 hours
Servings	**Nourish Points**
1 pouch	84 points

Ingredients

4 Trusty Milo™ Liquid Nutriment Packets
1 Trusty Milo™ Circle Foodstuff
½ Trusty Milo™ Authentic Mistletoe Prong
6 Trusty Milo™ Icy Squares (optional)

Instructions

1. Pour Liquid Nutriment Packets into large glassware or pouch. Add Authentic Mistletoe Prong. Soak overnight.
2. The next day, crush Circle Foodstuff until soft.
3. Slowly add crushed Circle Foodstuff into Liquid Nutriment Packet and Authentic Mistletoe Prong mixture.
4. Add Icy Squares if available at your local depot.
5. Best served in genuine glassware. If you have failed to earn your own, a liquid pouch may be used.

Recipe Notes

The Authentic Mistletoe Prong should dissolve in the Liquid Nutriment Packets overnight. If the Authentic Mistletoe Prong does not dissolve, do not consume the mixture. Consumption of improperly dissolved prongs may result in death and is the fault of the individual, not Trusty Milo™.

Howdy! My name is Abby Adams, and I'm here to spice up your nourishment package! I like to consider myself the top dog of nutri-babes, as confirmed by my two Trusty Milo™ Nourish Awards, but you can just consider me your friendly guide to trustworthy and safe meals!

Nutrition Facts

Trusty Milo™'s Original Merry Mistletoe Moonshine for Authentic Holiday Cheer

Amount Per Serving (1 pouch)

Nourish Points 84	Nourish Points from Trusty Milo™ Nutrients 84
	% Daily Value*
Fat 1p	**100%**
Sodium 1p	**100%**
Wellness Compound 1p	**100%**
Fiber 1p	**100%**
Protein 1p	**100%**

* Percent Daily Values are based on the Trusty Milo™ Nourish Everyone plan.

The Longest Night

by Maria Berejan

Jonathan picked the last of the mistletoe and frowned. He hoped it would be enough. He looked around the frosty wilderness before him and squinted up at the sky. No, there was no more time. He was late enough already, and there was no more mistletoe in sight. His stash would have to do.

He started the trek back through the snow-laden forest, heading wide around the mountain so he could hit Old Man Jagenbert's property on the way home. Old 'Bert was the closest Jonathan had to a neighbor, though the man's farmhouse was still a good mile downhill from his own modest cabin. One might think with the distance between them they'd hardly see each other, but in fact it was hard not to mingle. When you were the closest each other had to civilization, you tended to stick together, to mix wisdom and supplies if nothing else. This time, Jonathan was after a bit of both.

He got there within half an hour, eyes peeled for more mistletoe but seeing none, except for what hung on Jagenbert's own home. He knocked on the door and waited for the barking to subside. Ever since Jagenbert's wife died a couple of years ago, the man had collected strays like knickknacks. Now he had so many animals that Jonathan thought it bordered on hoarding at times, but it wasn't his place to judge an old man's comfort.

"Aye," came the hoarse voice from inside, right before the door opened to show a lean man behind it, skin aged and hardened like leather. Watery blue eyes peered up at him from beneath gray caterpillar brows grown wild with age. Jagenbert cleared his throat. "Jonathan, lad. Bit late, innit?" The man looked around warily. "It's not a good day to be out. You'd best come in."

Jonathan eyed the panting mutts at Jagenbert's heels. "That's alright. I've only got a minute." His hands tightened on his satchel straps, worrying the cloth. "I just—"

"Ah." The old man peered down at his satchel. "I see you took my advice. Got everything ready for tonight, have you?"

Jonathan shuffled uncomfortably. He wasn't one for folklore normally, but mountain life had its own way of catching up with you. He figured at worst this was just some extra safeguarding, and with young kids, you could never be too safe. "I've got the mistletoe here. You said I needed holy water, too. Did you happen to get any extra from your trek to town last week?"

Old Man Jagenbert nodded and shuffled inside, leaving a few hounds peeking out of the open door in his wake. A moment later he was back, a well-used plastic bottle in his hand, with the label peeled off.

Jonathan took it, almost expecting to feel some holy presence when he touched it, but it just weighed in his hand like any water bottle did. He tried not to feel stupid as he shoved it in his bag. "Thanks," he said, raising the corner of his bag in acknowledgement.

Old Man Jagenbert watched him with piercing eyes. Maybe it was Jonathan's imagination, but they looked sadder than usual, somehow haunted.

"Just take care of yourself, lad. Soak the leaves well, and get them all hung up before night sets. Won't go awry laying salt down, either." He looked up at the sky, gauging the time. "You'd best hurry home."

"Aye, sir," Jonathan said, turning to go, but a firm grip on his elbow stopped him. He turned back and met the old man's gaze.

"Remember, Jonathan. Every window, every door. The chimney, too. You mustn't let anything in tonight, alright? All it takes is once, Jonathan! Once they're in—just enough to leave something of themselves in there—they'll keep coming back, lad, over and over again, and you won't ever get them back out," Jagenbert said, and Jonathan involuntarily shivered.

"Alright." He hiked his satchel up higher on his shoulder and headed down the porch.

"Lock everything up tight!" Jagenbert called. Jonathan looked back at the man in the door, back hunched with age, a dog by his feet. Mistletoe above him and in every window he saw. Not for the first time, he wondered what he'd gotten himself into.

He raised a hand in farewell and saw one raised in return. Then, he turned and walked home, trying not to let the old man's words bother him.

———

"But *why* do we have to sleep in the basement tonight, daddy?" Timmy's voice said for the umpteenth time that day, the innocent lilt that only a four-year-old could truly pull off still in his voice.

"Because," Jonathan said, wringing out the last of the mistletoe from the holy water, "it'll be *exciting*. We'll all camp out and play games and fall asleep looking at the Christmas tree lights. Doesn't that sound fun?"

"It sounds fun," said Sam, his oldest, "but uncomfortable. And we all have to share the tent? You know, dad, you snore. Like, a lot."

"I'll sleep outside the tent, OK? And I'll give you earbuds," he said, and Sam rolled her eyes. That was her newest thing: the eye roll. He wasn't sure where she'd learned it from; it wasn't like there were other seven-year-olds on the mountain to guide her behavior.

"OK," he said. "How 'bout instead of the tent, we make a pillow fort?" Two pairs of eyes sparked with excitement before he even finished the sentence. Hook, line, and sinker. "You two go grab all the pillows and blankets you can find and get them downstairs. I'll meet you there as soon as I finish up here, and we'll get the party started," he said, and Timmy cheered.

"What are you doing up here?" Sam questioned, ever the astute one.

Jonathan looked at the mass of mistletoe bunches before him and wrinkled his nose. "Decorating. Here," he said, grabbing two of the sprigs. He pinned one to Sam's headband and the other to Timmy's shirt. "And now you two are ready. Keep those on, OK? Legend has it they'll keep you safe and warm. Christmas magic." He winked and saw Timmy's eyes go wide as the full moon.

"But where's yours, daddy?" Timmy asked.

"I'll get one later." Jonathan said, waving the question off. "Come on, now. Let's go!"

He watched his kids sprint off to gather the fort materials, and then he sighed and rubbed his face. He looked at the mass of greenery before him, and the absurdity of the situation crept back once more. There was no way this was real, and he was foolish for indulging in an old man's fables, but there was no harm in doing so, was there? None besides feeling dumb.

He went and grabbed a bag of salt, gathered up his freshly blessed mistletoe, and then he began. He started at the chimney first, remembering Old Man Jagenbert's warning. He strung up a branch of mistletoe as high as he could reach inside, and then on the perimeter of the fireplace, he carefully drew a thick, uninterrupted line of salt from end to end.

On he went to each windowsill and door. Mistletoe up; line of salt down.

He stopped just short of the last room, taking a deep breath as he stared at the closed door. This was her room, and he hadn't been in there since. He looked down at the last mistletoe in his hand and shook his head. There was nothing for it; he had to go in now.

He opened the door, keeping his eyes resolutely locked on the window on the opposite wall. He hung up the mistletoe and carefully drew the salt line.

"Dad?" came Sam's voice, and he looked back to see his daughter hovering in the doorway, Timmy hot on her heels. He strapped a smile to his face.

"Hey, guys. I'm just finishing now," he said, putting the rest of the salt bag in his pocket and heading back to the doorway.

Sam looked at the salt line on the windowsill and then at him. He saw the question in her eyes, but she didn't voice it, so he didn't answer. Instead, she said, "Can we take that blanket, too?" and pointed back behind him.

Jonathan blinked and looked back. Near the window he'd just vacated lay a neatly folded shawl — their mother's favorite. "Sure," he said, pushing down the feeling of discomfort that reared up his throat. "Sure, go right ahead." He swallowed and stepped out of her way. As he watched his daughter enter the room, he felt a great need to be anywhere but there.

"Come on. Let's go make some hot cocoa," he said, grabbing an eager Timmy by the hand and dragging him to the kitchen. He made the cocoa under Timmy's attentive gaze, and by the time they made it down to the basement, Sam was already there, propping pillows in a wide circle for the blanket fort. The Christmas tree was lit, and he'd strung up lights on the ceiling earlier in the week, so it looked like a bright night sky above them. All in all, it was rather cozy; not the worst way to spend a night.

He set the cups down and backtracked up the stairs, taking one last look out the window at the rapidly dimming sky. Tonight was the winter solstice; they were in for the longest night of the year. He did a quick glance around from his perch on the stairs, noting all the mistletoe one last time, and then shut the door. It was time to get these silly stories out of his head; this was a night like any other, and he was going to make the most of it with his kids.

They built the biggest fort they could and gorged on hot cocoa and sandwiches and spiced orange slices. They played *Go Fish* and told stories and crafted popcorn stringers for the tree, and by the time they were plumply satiated and bone-weary, Jonathan had all but forgotten why they were down there in the first place.

He was dozing when he felt someone shuffle next to him and opened his eyes to see Sam softly illuminated by the dim fairy lights. Timmy lay in the fort, fast asleep and drooling.

"Hey, kiddo. What's up?" he asked, his voice still a bit groggy, even as a whisper.

Sam shuffled a bit. "I miss mom."

Jonathan felt the words stab his heart like an icicle. "I know, darling. Me too."

"She should be here."

"I know," Jonathan said, reaching over to hug Sam. "Christmas was her favorite time of year."

Sam nodded and hugged back. And then, as seven-year-olds often do, she held out her hand with no warning, veering the conversation in a completely different direction. "Here," she said, and plopped something light and leathery in his hand. Jonathan's brain hiccupped, and he took a moment to reply.

"Where did you get this?" He stared numbly down at the mistletoe in his hand, and then looked up, checking her headband, but her mistletoe was still firmly in place.

"I thought you should have one, too," Sam said, which, while incredibly sweet, frustratingly did nothing to answer his question.

"Sam, that's lovely, darling, but I don't need one. Where did you get it?"

"Mama's room," Sam whispered, and Jonathan's blood seemed to freeze for an instant before rushing all at once to his ears.

He checked his wristwatch; it was almost midnight.

"Sam, I'm gonna go put this back, OK? I need you to stay here," he said quietly, grasping her shoulders to make sure she was listening. "Stay here with Timmy. I'll be back in just a little while, OK? But no matter what, you and Timmy are not to come out of this room before the sun comes up, OK? 8 a.m. — little hand on the eight, big hand on 12," he said, showing her on the watch.

"But — daddy — " Sam was frowning, shaking her head. She only called him daddy when she was worried. Most of the time she said she was too big for that sort of stuff.

"Sam, just listen to me, OK? Nothing's gonna happen, I promise, but I need to go put this back, and

I need you to not move. Just stay here and go to sleep, and I'll be back before you know it." He kissed her on the head and tucked her in before grabbing his flashlight and standing up. "Love you. I'll be right back," he said, keeping his voice level and stride smooth.

As soon as he was on the other side of the door, he took the hallway in galloping leaps. He heard the grandfather clock from the living room chime midnight as he approached the room, its door still ajar from earlier. He turned the flashlight on and waved it about, but nothing looked out of the ordinary.

He made his way to the windowsill, flashlight casting long dark shadows before him. The room was icy cold and the window panes frosted, and he felt the hairs on his neck begin to stand on end.

With one of his shirtsleeves, he wiped the fog away from the glass. He took a shuddering breath and peered out into the darkness.

There was nothing.

He sighed with relief he hadn't known he was missing and leaned back. What a foolish notion to begin with. He clenched his hand, crumpling the mistletoe, and shook his head. Of course there was nothing out there; nothing more than usual, to be sure. He'd go back down to his children and sleep, and tomorrow he'd clean everything up, and that would be that. He'd tell Jagenbert they'd slept like babes on feather-down pillows, no thanks to these outlandish superstitions. In fact, he had half a mind to tell the old man exactly where he could shove his mistletoe.

He chuckled to himself and glanced back up.

His eyes met a face. Its eyes stared straight back at his through the glass, whites gleaming and pale skin pressed close to the pane, inches from his own.

He cursed, jumping back, and tripped over the edge of a chair. His flashlight crashed to one side, and the mistletoe to the other.

Cursing again, he grasped at the floor like a drunkard, patting until he found the light and tapped it back on. It buzzed, flickering, before it came back.

As soon as it did, he pointed it right at the window, but nothing was there besides darkness.

He took a long breath in, shakily pulling himself to his feet and swinging the light around.

The once pristine salt line was interrupted, a large gash cutting through it. Frowning, he shoved the flecks back in place, his eye lingering once more on the darkness beyond the window glass, but it was just that—darkness. Nothing more.

Jonathan turned and flashed his light on the ground, searching for the mistletoe. He found it in a corner and reached for it, grabbing it just as his light illuminated a pair of feet right next to it, skin blackened and shriveled from frost.

His breath came in short bursts, and he felt himself hyperventilating as if from a great distance.

He moved the light up and looked directly into the face of what once was his wife. She was dead, and she looked it, her hands blackened and skin a violent, purplish blue.

It took a second for Jonathan's brain to catch up, but when it did, he scrambled away from her, toward the door. His hand shook, making the light quiver, but he kept it trained on her as best he could, hardly daring to blink, as if she would appear right next to him if he did.

But she didn't. She watched him go, head turning after him, as if it was his turn to act first.

He made it halfway to the open doorway before she began moving, taking a step forward and then another, stiffly, as if she were still getting used to the muscles she now possessed, but not slow enough for Jonathan's liking. He stumbled backward until his back hit the doorframe.

He didn't know where the thought came from, but in his state of panic and shock, his mind turned to Timmy and Sam in the basement. Had he closed the basement door when he'd left? He couldn't remember.

He stood frozen, watching this dead embodiment of his wife step closer, reaching for him with mangled claws, and he knew he had no choice.

He slammed the door closed, so neither of them could get out, and took the last of the salt out of his pocket, drawing a shaky but solid half circle around him and the door, as far away from himself as his arms could reach. Then he held his crumpled mistletoe out before him like one would a cross to a monster.

She stopped just short of it, watching him.

He watched her back, his light trembling, casting shadows on her face.

She slowly paced around the line, but came no closer. He watched her take every step with bated breath.

And so, their stalemate began.

———

This was the room where she'd killed herself, his Esther. It had been shortly after last Christmas, which he'd never understood because she'd always loved Christmas. *Stove, sweater, and mistletoe weather* she'd call it, and bundle up so much that most days Jonathan would only ever see the tip of her head.

He remembered coming into the room and seeing her sitting on the chair—the same one she was standing beside now—only she'd been reading then, wrapped up in the shawl Sam had taken earlier that day. She'd smiled. She'd held up some mistletoe, a mischievous flicker in her eyes and on her lips—and oh, how he'd loved those lips. He hadn't been able to resist kissing her, smelling the scent of her, feeling her hair tickle his cheek.

The light had come in through the window—chilly rays of winter sunlight, but those always seemed to warm them up the most. They'd basked in the light and smiled at each other, before she'd gently pulled away. He'd taken the kids out to cut some firewood and build snowmen. They were amassing a small army to guard their home. And then, when he'd come in later that day, she'd been in the same spot still, head resting on her hand, staring out of the window.

Only she hadn't been staring. Not really. She'd already been dead, the pill bottles empty in her lap next to the mistletoe sprig she'd used as a bookmark, on top of her still-open book.

He'd wished for the past year he could see her again, feel her, be with her. Now, as he stared into the dark, dead eyes staring right back into his own, he wished he would never see her again.

———

"Daddy?" Sam's voice came through the door behind him, wavering slightly. Jonathan took a shaky breath in himself. Esther watched him from across the salt line, unblinking.

"Yes, darling?" Jonathan tried to keep his voice level.

"Daddy, are you OK?" He felt a pang at making her so scared.

"Yes, honey, I'm fine. Just a little…busy," he said, not taking his eyes off of his dead wife for even a moment. "I thought I told you not to come out until morning."

"Big hand on the eight and little on the 12," Sam's voice came through, muffled by the door.

"Other way around, honey."

"Oh," she said. "Daddy, come out."

"I'm sorry, honey." Jonathan clenched his fists. His breath came out in a fog, and his knees trembled together. The temperature in the room had begun to drop and seemed to be steadily continuing as long as she was there. "In the morning. I'll come out in the morning."

"But daddy—"

"I love you, honey."

"I love you, too."

———

At some point through the night, his flashlight began dimming and then slowly gave out, pitching him into bitter darkness. He shook the light, slapping it against his thigh, as if that would do anything. He knew it wouldn't, but it was calming to think otherwise—to at least be trying to do something rather than sitting there doing nothing as his extremities slowly froze.

In the dark, and from a distance, he could almost forget the monster before him and remember the woman he'd once loved. The slenderness of her form. The cascade of loose curls down her back. The distinct sound of her footsteps, her own signature dance across the floorboards. Those footsteps had tormented his dreams for a year now, their absence a jarring ache in his life.

He couldn't help the broken whisper that escaped him hours into the night. "Why?" he asked. His voice trembled with more than just cold. "Why did you do it?"

Esther looked at him, her eyes dark and unfathomable. But then the shadows on her face changed, and her expression seemed to flicker.

Jonathan blinked, his tired eyes trying to make sense of what they saw.

She leaned close to the salt line — to him — as close as she could get. With bated breath, Jonathan inched closer too, as if drawn by a magnet. His body buzzed with excitement and confusion as he waited for the answer to fall off her lips.

Instead she lunged, hands held like talons before her and face twisted into a vicious, silent snarl.

Jonathan flew back just in time; her sharp claws clipped some hairs from his beard, but nothing more before he brandished the mistletoe like a weapon in front of him, forcing her to retreat.

She did so with a low growl, settling back down in her sentry position opposite his.

Her black eyes watched his, never blinking. Waiting for his next mistake.

———

Sam had stopped shifting back and forth on the other side of the door. He'd told her to go back down to sleep long ago, of course, but she had ignored him, pretending not to hear. Now her soft breathing came through the door, even and deep, and it made him feel better that at least she wasn't sitting out there scared shitless anymore.

His eyes tracked Esther as she paced around the room, checking for gaps in his protective lines and scratching at walls and floorboards. He marked her by the whites of her eyes; sometimes she'd veer off to a corner, barely visible, and other times she'd come so close he could feel her breath surround him, putrid with the rot of death.

He was tired now. So tired, and so cold. His eyes burned, every moment they remained open a battle of will that he wasn't sure he could keep up for much longer. He kept his arm out straight, holding the mistletoe aloft. His toes and fingers had hurt before, but now they were so cold they'd gone numb. He'd stopped shaking, too. He couldn't feel much of anything anymore.

But he watched, and he waited, counting time down in his head. Whatever it was, it felt like more.

He waited for dawn to come.

———

He must have dozed off for a second, for he woke with a start, his body in panic mode. He looked around wildly, reaching for the light before his brain caught up with his body and reminded him it was useless for more than one reason: dawn light was already trickling in through the window. The salt line around him was undisturbed. The mistletoe remained in his hand, and there was no sign of Esther around.

Jonathan gulped large breaths of air, stumbling to his deadened feet and staggering toward the window. He stuck his head out, looking all around, but there were no signs of anything and no tracks leading away. If he didn't know better, he thought he might have dreamt the whole thing—then again, had he? He didn't remember opening the window.

"Daddy?" Sam's voice came from the other side of the door, plunging him back to reality. "Daddy, can I come in now? It's morning."

"And I'm hungry!" Timmy's voice came as well.

Jonathan frowned. He closed the window and stepped back, turning in a slow circle and surveying the room before him. He tried to recall what Old Man 'Bert had told him the day before. The memories surfaced slowly, as though from a lifetime ago. Nothing looked amiss.

"Dad," Sam's voice came again, impatiently now.

"Yeah, guys, I'm coming out now," he said and shook his head. He suddenly felt very tired. He'd go and talk to Old Man 'Bert after breakfast, he decided. For now, he had to deal with the living.

He plastered a smile on his face and unlocked the door, meeting his children's hugs with an enthusiasm that bordered on fervor. He hadn't realized how worried he'd been until he had them in his arms, warm and solid and safe. They'd done it; they'd survived. They'd be OK.

"Come on," he said, his smile real now as he grabbed each child by a hand. "Let's go make pancakes."

Timmy nodded vigorously, tugging Jonathan toward the kitchen, and Jonathan laughed louder than he had in a good long time. He looked back, where Sam was gathering up the pillow she'd used and

Esther's blanket. Jonathan felt a pang he was too tired to analyze. "Sam, you coming?"

"Yep. Just gonna put this stuff away," she called back, and Jonathan wondered, not for the first time, when she'd become so grown-up. He felt another tug on his arm and turned toward the ravenous four-year-old before him.

"Come *on*, daddy!" Timmy urged, and Jonathan chuckled, letting the young boy lead the way.

———

Sam watched them go as she finished folding the blanket and slowly stepped into the room. She looked around, wondering why her dad had holed himself up in here the night before. She'd heard movement, and whispers, and crying. She wondered if he'd had a bad dream.

She went to the chair in the corner and carefully placed the folded blanket over the backrest. On the seat cushion was her mother's book, just as it had been the day before, but now there was something on top. She recognized it in an instant; she'd seen it many times before.

She picked up her mother's wedding ring and held it close. Where it had rested, it left a small, crimson circle.

She hesitated a moment, then placed the ring in her pocket and flipped the book over to hide the smudge. Maybe she'd ask about it another day. For now, she had a plate of pancakes calling her name.

To Give and To Receive

by Stephen Folkins

Annie was gathering her things to get out of the car, but Hector tugged playfully at her sleeve.

"We don't have to go in right away," he said. He raised his eyebrows twice in succession.

"It's snowing out. We'll get cold." She was so close to her goal. She'd hoped there wouldn't have to be a one last time.

Hector draped a long, muscled arm over her shoulder. "I'll keep you warm, baby."

"Aww, you," she said, sighing. "Fine then." She just had to get him inside the party, and it would all be worth it. Camarin had promised her that she'd be able to get her hands on some.

Hector grinned like a kid being given a treat. He was tall, handsome in a stretched-out way, with a square jaw lightly covered in gold peach fuzz. He was the all-American golden boy you made your final decision about somewhere between second and third base. She'd lusted after him for two years before that bitch Amber opened her big mouth and Annie's secret crush got out. Of course, it turned out that he was quite taken with the idea of someone having a crush on him, so she couldn't be too mad at Amber. That bitch.

Now he was all hers.

And here he came, revealing the one flaw she could never have foreseen.

He was a monumentally bad kisser.

His cold, wet lips met hers with no force behind them, and he moved his head side to side from his neck, creating a weird torque that pressed one half of her mouth up and the other down.

His arms were solid and held her gently. His hand rested against her back, his thumb drawing small, comforting circles. His breath was fresh and minty.

But, Jesus Christ, she could feel his teeth through both their lips. What was he even getting out of this? Was this pleasant for him?

He transitioned into giving her a series of pecks on the lips, making a little smack each time. She'd tried to lead by example before, but he didn't seem to have any sensation in his lips at all.

She had tested this theory by biting him pretty hard one time. It turned out that he absolutely could feel her biting down on his lip. He was pretty upset, but at least it had brought that particular necking session to a close.

This was the last time, though. She'd asked Camarin how much money she should bring, and Cam had said just a dollar. That seemed way too low for anything effective, but she had too much riding on this now for doubts.

Hector pulled away, breathing heavily, and caressed her cheek in satisfaction. "Want to keep going a little longer?"

"Later," she said, "if you're good." She tapped his nose. He grinned. He derived some measure of pleasure from being teased, so she'd been able to limit the makeouts without feeling too withholding. But everything would change tonight. "Come on. Let's go in."

———

"Annie! Come in!" Tony's mom gave her a hug. "And let me get your coat. Hector, nice to see you. Me and Bob were cheering for you at the swim meet."

"Thanks, Mrs. Capatelli." Hector helped Annie take off her coat and handed it to the hostess. He had braved the cold with just a sweater.

"The kids are downstairs," Mrs. Capatelli said. "Why don't you grab some cider and go join them? We'll all meet up here when it's time for carols."

"That sounds great, Mrs. Capatelli. Thanks." Annie let herself be guided to the kitchen, making small talk about her parents and little brother, but her mind was already downstairs. "Hey, Mrs. Capatelli, has Camarin gotten here yet?"

"Oh, she got here just a minute before you, sweetheart. I'm surprised you didn't run into each other at the door."

Damn it. If she'd just seen Camarin, she could have begged off that last kiss. But no matter; that was in the past. This party was about the future.

Cider in hand, they made their way downstairs. Mrs. Capatelli walked heavily on the steps, giving the teens below an opportunity to get out of any compromising positions.

Everyone shouted "Hey!" when they appeared. The teens were all sitting around a TV where the

Grinch was stealing Christmas. Several couples were cuddled under blankets, but all hands were visible over the covers, so the warning had done its job.

Annie spotted Camarin sitting between Tony's legs and gave her a questioning look.

Camarin smiled: *yes*.

Relief flooded over Annie. Her long, clammy nightmare was at an end.

They sat down and chatted with a few acquaintances, talking over the old, familiar cartoon until Camarin plopped down on Annie's lap, forcing the air out of her.

"Jesus Christ," Annie said with what breath was left. "How old are you?"

"Old enough to have a bag of new and exotic drugs in my left pocket."

Annie couldn't help looking for the telltale lump, and Camarin smiled kindly. "I know how much you've needed this. Let's all go to Tony's room."

Camarin took off, and Annie turned to Hector. He looked leery when she grabbed his hands and pulled him in, but when she whispered that they should find somewhere more private, he was up in a flash and leading the way.

———

Camarin threw her dry, dirty blonde braid over her shoulder and launched into her spiel.

"In the jungles of South America, the natives will drink juice from the ayahuasca leaf to give themselves spiritual visions. It's said that these visions reveal knowledge about the universe hidden deep within you. After taking the drug, the natives would draw from what they saw, revealing DNA double helices and cellular mitosis centuries before they'd be discovered by science. This" — she dramatically pulled a baggie out of her left pocket, a mass of green inside — "is the key to unlocking the hidden potential inside you. When we use this together, we will learn what we have always known." Camarin waved her hands mysteriously, and Annie waved at her to get on with it.

"Cool. What is it?" Hector asked, game as ever.

Camarin shook the stuff out of the baggie, revealing a handful of oblong, rounded leaves.

"This" — she waved a hand over it — "is mistletoe."

"Isn't it supposed to be all spikey?" Annie asked, worried they'd been fooled.

"That's holly leaves, dork," Tony said, getting a small cylinder out of the drawer on his bedside table.

Hector punched him on the arm only a little harder than if he were kidding. "Don't call my girlfriend a dork."

"Shut up, dorks," Camarin snapped. "This is serious business. It's not like salvia, or pot, or whatever those pills were that Amber stole from her mom's purse. It's a delicate process." She took the cylinder from Tony, popped the lid off, and stuffed the mistletoe inside.

"What's it do?" Hector asked, his curiosity finally catching up to the conversation.

"It makes kissing feel amazing." Camarin smiled and started slapping the cylinder.

"What are you doing?" Annie asked. "That's not how grinders work."

"It's not a grinder. It's a slap chop. Grinding only works for dried leaves, and these have to be wet still." She continued to finely dice the leaves until they broke down into a sandy-looking slurry.

"And how do we take it?" Hector asked. Annie felt a little bad that he was the only one in the dark about this whole thing. But it was for the best. He would thank her once he was good at kissing. In fact, as she had no illusions about staying together past graduation, a whole bunch of girls would thank her for this. All she asked was a year of this. One year with a sweet, pretty boyfriend who wasn't god-awful at kissing.

"You snort it," Tony said, hanging his arm over Camarin's shoulders.

"But it's not going to be a powder."

"Doesn't matter. You still gotta snort it. Trust me: you don't want it in your mouth."

Camarin decided the leaves were about as slushy as they'd get and used an eye dropper to extract and pour out four lines of viscous goo onto a CD case.

"Okay. One for everyone," she said.

"I don't know if I actually need one," Hector said. "I already can't imagine anything better than kissing Annie."

"Aww," Tony and Camarin both cooed, taken by his sweetness—but they wouldn't have been charmed by it if they'd ever had to kiss him.

"Come on. It's Christmas," Annie said, as if that was some kind of winning argument. She held the CD case out to him. "Does he need a straw or something?"

"Nope," Camarin said. "Just put a nostril at one end and the rest will follow."

"Well, it *is* Christmas, I guess," Hector said, convinced. He downed the rest of his cider and leaned over the proffered lines of snot. He placed one nostril over the nearest line, covered the other, and took a big old sniff.

It looked like blowing your nose in reverse. First the near end of the line jumped up and adhered to Hector's nose, and then the rest contracted like elastic and snapped up into the awaiting orifice.

Hector's head jerked back, and he smacked his lips a few times in distaste.

"How do you feel?" Annie asked,

"Like I immediately want to blow my nose," Hector answered. Annie gave an uncertain look to Camarin, but her friend calmly nodded to continue. If this was all some kind of joke, she'd have to break up with Hector tonight. She couldn't take any more of his dead-fish kisses. This had to work.

Annie leaned over the CD case and pressed her nostril against the second line. There was still a sticky green residue from where Hector's line had been sucked up. She covered one nostril and went for broke.

Her first impulse was to immediately sneeze and never stop. Anything to get rid of what could only be a parasite crawling into her sinuses.

Then a bitter taste developed at the back of her throat as some of the goop cleared as drainage.

Then nothing in particular. Her nose was a bit uncomfortable, but nothing seemed different otherwise.

Tony and Camarin took their lines with practiced efficiency, smiled at each other, and immediately began kissing like a couple reunited at the end of a movie.

"You ready?" Hector asked her, squaring his face up as always, his bottom lip hanging open with his chin extended.

"I hope so," she said.

Annie grabbed the back of Hector's neck and pulled him into the best kiss she could muster.

And was met with a slack pair of lips pushed perpendicular to hers. Hector worked his jaw like a trout, and tears welled in Annie's eyes. This was the end. She would have to break up with him and never tell him why.

But then Hector's lips pursed, growing firm and brushing over hers. They parted slightly and then gave, rising again to meet her in a real kiss. They moved in time, falling into each other's rhythms. Every once in a while, one of them would intensify the kiss, pulling in harder and for longer, before releasing again and resuming the cycle.

Soft bites interspersed. The occasional exploratory tip of the tongue. It was like nothing Annie had ever known. She was exquisitely aware of every moment, but before she knew it, a half hour had passed.

The partygoers in the other room exploded into a muffled exclamation over something or other, and Annie pulled herself reluctantly away from Hector. They met each other's eyes and laughed a little. Tony and Camarin were still going at it.

She took Hector's hand in hers and squeezed it gently.

"You want to take a little walk?" Hector asked.

"That'd be great." She leaned in for another brief kiss, just as thrilling for its fleeting moment. They did not bother to interrupt Tony and Camarin with their departure.

———

The air was dry and chilly, now that the snow had let up. It was refreshing, and Annie could feel her cheeks tingling as she walked hand in hand with Hector down the sidewalk, idly taking in the ostentatious Christmas decorations on the neighbors' houses.

Every few steps, it felt like Hector was trying to shake her hand off or squeezing it weirdly. Something was wrong.

"That mistletoe stuff was pretty good, huh?" she said.

"Oh my God, yeah." Hector said. "That was probably some of the best kissing we've ever done."

"I couldn't agree more," Annie said, slyly, but then Hector unclasped his hand from hers and started messing with his knit cap.

"Is everything okay?" Annie asked, sensing he was working himself up to something.

He turned to face her head-on, and her vision tunneled. This wasn't right at all.

"Annie, I think we need to break up."

Annie took a moment to collect herself before responding.

"You're fucking kidding me," Annie said.

"I've been feeling this way for a while," Hector said, suddenly speaking very quickly, eager to get it all out now that he'd worked himself up. "You're really great. Really. It's just that, with college applications due, and my mom really wants me to do the Harvard Model Congress — "

"You're fucking kidding me," Annie said, slower and more forcefully.

"I mean, we're not even applying to any of the same schools. It's not like we were going to — "

"Not the issue," Annie snapped. "Why? Why do you want to break up? Is it someone else? Is it Marcy?"

"No, no, it's nothing like that. I didn't even know Marcy liked me."

"I swear to God, Hector. If you don't give me something solid right now, I'm going to claw your eyes out."

"No, I really feel like you'll be angrier if I tell you."

"Hector."

"You're really bad at holding hands, okay?" Hector exploded. He turned around, grabbed his head, and began pacing maniacally.

Annie let him stomp around and blow off steam until he came back to face her, red-faced and puffy-eyed.

"You're fucking kidding me," Annie said.

"I know what you're thinking," Hector interrupted. "This is not some bullshit excuse to dump you. I've tried everything. I got you all those lotions and creams and powders. I've tried wearing gloves. I've tried to just not hold your hand at all. But Annie, nothing works. It's like being grabbed by a skinned python that's trying to rhythmically crush you. Your hand feels like a sticky, pulsating heart that occasionally stabs me with jagged spikes. I have never once felt your hands dry. Sometimes your hand will go limp and cold, and I can feel it draining the heat out of my body like a ghost. You pinch the webbing between my thumb and index finger until the skin breaks. You literally broke my ring finger a month into our relationship."

Annie was horrified, and she tried to comfort Hector, but her first instinct — to grab his hands — was the wrong one.

"No! Annie, I can't take it. I know it's unfair. I know it seems like it shouldn't matter, but it does. It really does. It's like, you know how you never really think about your thumb until you get a cut on it, and then you suddenly realize how central your thumb is to everything you do? That's what it's been like dating you. I have never not known where your hands were for the past five months, lest they *get* me."

As tears began to fill Annie's eyes, he changed tack.

"Look, I'm sorry. I wish I could get over this, but I can't. Obviously, you're the nicest, prettiest girl I've ever met, and I couldn't believe my luck that I ended up with you. But I just can't take it anymore. I still want to be in your life. I still want to be your friend. I just can't touch your hands anymore."

As he ran out of steam, Annie was full-on ugly crying, snot running down her face, mouth pulled back into a rictus.

"Annie." Hector was filled with shame. "I'm so sorry. I should have just said something before letting it turn into a whole thing."

"It's not that," Annie whined, wiping her eyes. "I never realized. I'm just as bad as you." With that, she broke down completely into sobs and fell to her knees. Hector swooped down to hold her, but recoiled when she went to meet his hands. "This whole time, I thought you were the hopeless, disgusting one" — she was wracked by a few more sobs — "and that if I could just fix you, everything would be alright. But I never thought that I could be the same as you: totally oblivious that I was doing something absolutely repellant and nauseating. Like you!"

"Wait, what do I do that's like your hands?"

"You're a horrible kisser, Hector!"

"What? No. No way!" He laughed dismissively. "That doesn't...what're you...no way!"

"Yes, Hector, you are. For the longest time I assumed you had to be doing it on purpose. I swear you have tried to inhale my tongue multiple times."

"But we have a great time kissing. It's nice! It's sexy!"

"Maybe for you, but for me it's a fight for survival. I was so close to ending it so many times, but I never dreamed I was subjecting you to the same kind of hell."

"But you just said we did our best kissing ever."

"Yes, that's right! I had to take a drug specifically for kissing to keep dating you!"

Hector reddened further and was clearly about to refocus the conversation on her hand-holding when the unmistakable sound of a dog peeing loudly into the snow interrupted them.

They both looked away from each other to see a tiny Pomeranian unleashing a concerningly powerful stream of urine onto a pile of snow on the curb. Attached to his leash, a middle-aged woman watched them with interest. She shrugged at their regard and turned to watch her dog perform its extended business as if she were no longer listening.

The dog had no such compunction and stared shamelessly, one rear leg pointed at them in silent accusation.

They waited far too long for the dog to finish its micturition and watched as the lady took the hint and walked the little fluff ball out of earshot.

"Annie, I'm so sorry. I had no idea. Why didn't you say anything?"

"The same reason you didn't. How do you bring that up?"

"You're right. You're right." Hector scratched his head helplessly.

"So that's it? We're done?"

"I mean, now that it's all out in the open, we could work on ourselves and try to get past these issues together?"

"My issue is solved, though," Annie laughed joylessly. "I've got the mistletoe if I ever don't like your kissing." She looked up at him, eyes filling again with tears. "And I don't think Camarin has any drugs for hand-holding?"

"Drugs for hand-holding?" Camarin shouted from the porch back across the street, where she'd been watching their conversation, lit cigarette in hand.

"Jesus, Cam," Annie startled. "How long have you been there?"

"Pretty much the whole time." She leaned forward onto the porch railing with a grin. "One of the side effects of the mistletoe is that it makes you compulsively confess things, so I had to get away from Tony while he came down."

"So you came out here to watch us confess things?" Hector demanded.

"Yes," Camarin said, giving a thumbs-up.

"Forget about it," Annie said. "You said there are drugs to help me hold hands?"

"Oh yeah." Camarin threw the butt of her cigarette into the snow, producing a satisfying hiss. "Drugs for hand-holding. You're actually asking at the perfect time. So, you know those conversation hearts candies?"

Snowball Fights and Thursday Nights

by Shay Lynam

When I was younger, I used to drop my backpack on the floor as soon as I got home from school every day and run back outside before my mom could stop me. I'd spend all afternoon wandering in the woods behind my house, pretending I was Princess Callie, a lost royal off on an adventure, or Captain Callie, the notorious pirate thief evading those trying to capture me.

I couldn't tell you now what I was pretending to be on the day I stumbled upon a boy sitting on a fallen log with his head in his hands. It was obvious he was crying, despite his best efforts to hide it. It's hard to hide tears when they've left clean streaks down your dirty face.

At first he refused to tell me what was wrong, but with some nagging, I finally got him to admit that he'd caught the back pocket of his jeans on a tree branch and ripped it clean off. Of course, I wouldn't believe him until he stood up and showed me, and when he did, I laughed at him. But with his Spider-Man underwear on full display, could you really blame me?

He got pretty mad, but I still managed to convince him to come back to my house with me. He wore a pair of my pink sweats while my mom sewed the pocket back on his jeans.

That was the day Jake Preston became my best friend.

———

Twelve years later, I once again make my way through the woods, only now I'm much older and much less agile. There's also about two feet of snow covering everything. Maybe it wasn't the best plan in the world, but the moment I looked up to see flakes falling outside my window and remembered that Jake was home for winter break, I just knew I had to pay him a visit, if for no other reason than to peg him in the face with a snowball.

By the time I break out of the forest and onto the somewhat plowed path leading into Jake's neighborhood, my pants are soaked up past my knees, and I can't feel my fingers.

His bedroom window is at the back of his house, and when I get to the gate leading into the backyard, I have to reach over and feel around until I find the latch. The swing set is still there, unused for who knows how many years now. I imagine it's all rusted and broken under that layer of snow. I figured his parents would have gotten rid of it by now, but I'm glad they haven't. Some of our best conversations were had while swinging back and forth together in the dark. It was where I learned about his dreams of becoming a screenwriter, where he listened to me cry after my first real breakup.

Where I realized I was in love with my best friend.

A smile pulls the corners of my mouth as I bend down and start gathering snow, packing it into a ball.

The two of us have gotten so close over the years because of that swing set, and yet I've never told him how I really feel. I would rather have my best friend than risk the heartache of rejection anyway. Then again, I have noticed subtle differences in recent years. Lingering hugs. A sudden interest in my dating life. But then again, maybe I'm just delusional in my desire for something more.

With a sigh to clear the thoughts away, I aim for the window. But I'm concentrating too much on perfecting my angle of trajectory and don't notice the window open or the familiar face looking back at me. By the time I do, the snowball is already airborne.

"Callie? What are you—hey!"

I don't even try to contain my laughter as Jake paws at his face and shirt, trying to get rid of the icy snow before it soaks in.

"Was that really necessary?" he hisses.

It takes me a minute to get my breath back. "I didn't know you were going to open your window!"

"How else was I supposed to yell at you for coming over here in the middle of the night?"

"I *had* to come over," I reply. "It snowed!"

"I see that," Jake says. "Just give me a minute." He disappears back inside, pulling his window shut.

A few minutes later, he joins me outside; his hair is tucked up under a beanie, though a couple dark strands stick out, still damp. I purse my lips to try and keep from grinning too widely.

"Sorry about that," I say, even though we both know I'm not.

Jake scoffs and looks up at the trees lining his back fence. "So, you're back."

"For a little while," I say. "I'm just on winter break. You?"

"Same."

Now what? It hadn't occurred to me that even though we text each other a lot, we haven't had any sort of in-person conversation in a while.

"Want to go for a walk?" Jake asks, the unease in his voice too obvious for either of us to ignore.

The thrill of both the initial trek to get here and managing to launch a snowball into his face has worn off, and I don't really know how to proceed.

Just say something!

"Sure," I blurt out.

It's strange walking down this road again. With the haze of the falling snow and the stark white against the shadowed houses, it feels more like I'm walking through an old photograph than my best friend's neighborhood. It looks different. Unfamiliar. Maybe because it's been so long.

With Jake going to community college a town over and me going out of state, we've kept up with each other's lives virtually, but of course it's not the same. Not when you're so used to seeing your best friend all the time. What used to be texts every day, continuing whatever conversation we were on the day before, has died down. Now it's just the odd message here and there, really only to talk about the newest episode of our favorite true crime podcast.

"So how's school going?" Jake finally asks once we've been walking in silence for half a block.

The laugh escapes before I can catch it, and Jake's head snaps up, eyes wide with confusion.

"Did you really just ask that?" I laugh. "We're both in college, Jake. It's going the same for me as it is for every other college student out there. I've changed my major twice already, am very much regretting signing up for that 8 a.m. class, and brought my laundry home for my mom to do it." A shy smile pulls at his mouth, and I swear I can see his cheeks turning red. "What you really should have asked," I continue, in hopes it'll take away the awkwardness, "is how the police could have *possibly* missed that it was Mr. Feeley the whole time." I catch Jake looking at me out of the corner of my eye. "I mean, *I* knew that from the get-go. What a letdown of a season finale."

"I haven't listened to it yet," Jake admits quietly, and now it's my turn to look at him with shock.

"You haven't?" I ask.

"No, I was sort of busy."

"Busy? You always listen to *Murder She Spoke* on Thursday nights."

"Yeah," Jake shrugs. "I was hanging out with someone, and I guess I sort of forgot about the season finale."

Realization hits me like a snowball to the face. "Oh," I say quickly. "Oh, you were on a date, weren't you? That's okay—I mean, that's good."

"Yeah," Jake says. "And I kept forgetting to listen to the episode. I planned on texting you, but—"

"No, it's okay," I interrupt, trying and failing to make it seem like it's not a big deal. "Um, how was it?"

"How was what?"

"Your date."

Jake shrugs. "It was alright, I guess. She was cool, but neither of us were really into it. I saw her at a party a couple nights after, and we talked a bit, but that's it."

"Oh, OK." I feel bad for the slight sense of relief blooming in my chest, especially since I've been going on dates as well. After all, Jake and I are only friends. I have no right to feel this way. Even if I couldn't stop thinking about him while I was on those dates....

Stop, Callie.

We spend the last bit of the walk in silence, Jake lost in thought and me berating myself for being such a jealous dork. Soon we reach the park at the end of the street, which was our second-favorite hangout spot when we were kids. The gazebo that stands in the middle started out as nothing more than a shelter for when it rained too hard to play on the playground, but over the years, it took on other, bigger roles.

Back then it was a mansion for us to pretend to live in, a hideout where we could avoid the imaginary police who were looking for us, a safe zone where the person who was "it" couldn't tag the other. Of course, that would then become a standoff while the non-"it" person caught their breath before making a mad dash out of there.

Now it stands in front of us in the dark, waiting like an old friend. Quite some time has passed since we've been here — years, actually — and now it looks so much smaller than it used to. Small enough that I have to duck my head to keep from hitting the icicles that hang from the edge of the roof as we step inside.

"Has this thing always been so dumpy?" Jake asks as he rubs his thumb over the peeling white paint on one of the posts.

"Come on," I say. "It's quaint."

"It's tiny."

"It's charming."

"It's falling apart."

The floor is slick, so I'm extra cautious as I make my way toward the center — which really only takes a couple steps to reach because, like Jake said, the thing is tiny.

"Dad told me the homeowners' association is planning on tearing it down in the spring," he says, also making his way carefully into the middle of the structure.

I let out a dramatic sigh. "I guess it's served its purpose." My eyes focus now on the rusting railings and rotting floorboards. Even if it is falling apart, I can't help but feel a twinge of sadness at the thought of no longer being able to come back here. "I think I might actually miss this thing once it's gone."

Jake smiles. "It's not like either of us have visited it recently."

"Well, now we won't even have the option." I cross my arms over my chest. "And here I thought the gazebo meant something to you."

A puff of air escapes his mouth as he chuckles at my obvious sarcasm. "You know it wasn't the gazebo that meant something to me."

Oh.

"Hey, Callie." Jake motions with his head for me to look up, and my eyes land on a clump of green, spiky leaves hanging from a red ribbon in the center of the gazebo. I feel my stomach drop a bit.

"Did you know mistletoe is poisonous?" I blurt.

Jake frowns. "Really?" He looks up at it again. "Leave it to humans to romanticize a deadly plant."

"Well, it's not deadly." I try to ignore the pounding of my heart in my ears. *It's a frickin' plant, Callie. Calm down.* "It can just make you sick. Like, a dizzy, barfing, seizing type of sick."

"How romantic."

"And that's not even mistletoe." I tilt my chin up at the plant. "It's holly."

Jake shakes his head. "Poisonous *and* deceptive."

"Um...all that aside" — I take a deep breath — "it is kind of a weird tradition, right?" My eyes sink to our feet. "I mean, why let a plant dictate when you kiss someone?"

"Eh, I kind of like it," Jake says with a shrug. "It's spontaneous and takes the pressure off."

And sometimes you really do need a silly reason to do something you have maybe been wanting to do for a long time now. "So, what you're saying," I reason, "is that if we didn't, that would be sort of like...slapping Christmas in the face, right?"

He sucks in a sharp breath. "Right." Why does his voice sound different all of a sudden? He sounds as nervous as I feel. "And we definitely wouldn't want to disrespect such a long-standing tradition."

"Right." Suddenly my knees feel weak. I still haven't taken my eyes off my shoes. I don't even know if I can muster up the nerve.

"Callie."

I look up.

He's so close now. His eyes look into mine, eyebrows furrowed just slightly with uncertainty. Neither of us moves for a moment. The air feels thick and warm, despite the fact that it's definitely below freezing. But here under the gazebo, the two of us are in our own little world — a world the cold can't penetrate.

"Hi," he says.

I swallow. "Hi."

My heart pounds in my ears. His mouth keeps coming closer, and my vision grows fuzzy as I try to focus on his face. I close my eyes just before his lips brush against mine.

At first, I think that's it. That it was a good enough kiss to fulfill the tradition. But then he steps closer so his chest presses against mine, and his hand comes up to cup the back of my neck, and oh — now we are *really* kissing.

I'm kissing him. I'm kissing my best friend. The boy I've been in love with for years and have cared about even longer. The boy who has let me cry on his shoulder over other boys, over my parents fighting, over having to put my cat Maisy down. He's kissing me now.

When at last he pulls back, I keep my eyes closed, afraid if I open them that the moment will be over. His hands slide up to hold either side of my face, and his forehead presses against mine, breath hot against my mouth. I can feel him staring at me, but I still don't open my eyes. I don't want to let go. I don't want the reason that he kissed me to be the stupid little plant hanging over our heads that isn't even technically mistletoe. I just want it to be real. And if I just keep my eyes closed, I can imagine that it is.

"Callie, look at me," Jake says.

I shake my head. "I don't want to." And then, much to my horror, I feel tears begin to prick at the corners of my eyes. I squeeze them shut tighter.

"Callie."

"Nope. Not opening them."

Jake chuckles and runs a thumb over my cheekbone, causing the fissure in my heart to grow. "Why not?"

"Because—" My breath hitches, and I have to take a second to catch it again. *This is mortifying.* "Because I'm not ready for this to be over yet."

"What makes you think it has to be over?"

What makes me think it has to be over? Because you're my best friend. Because I saw your Spider-Man underwear when we were eight. Because come spring, this gazebo is going to be torn down. Because there's a swing set in your backyard that is rusting and rickety from all the years we spent swinging on it. Because I don't want to lose you.

Finally, I open one eye, and his smile widens, causing his dimples to appear. I squeeze my eyes shut again. "Here's the thing, Jake," I say at last to the darkness. "I've liked you for a long time now. And I know that this whole mistletoe thing is just some silly Christmas tradition, and we were just being dorks—"

"You like me?"

I freeze. *Did I just make the biggest mistake of my life?* His hands are still warm against my cheeks, and if I really did just freak him out, he'd be halfway home already, right?

Cautiously, I open my eyes—both this time. Jake is still looking back at me, his own eyes darting back and forth as they search mine. I pull in a breath.

"Um, yeah, I do," I mutter.

"Seriously?"

I really did just screw this up, didn't I?

I take a step back and give a small nod. "Yeah, um, I do," I say. "But things don't have to be weird or anything," I add quickly. "I mean, I'm fine just being friends—I mean, I *like* just being friends—and you can go on dates with whoever, whenever. Not that you need my permission or anything, but we can just go on like this never happened and we can just talk about *Murder She Spoke*." I'm completely disconnected from my body at this point—just floating above us, watching this dumpster fire continue to burn, and I can't seem to do anything about it. "Oh, right, you haven't listened to the newest one yet—well, when you do, you can just, like, let me know—or not, if this is all too weird to you. I can just go home if you want, and we can just pretend—"

"Callie."

In that moment I crash back down into my body and stumble back against the railing, holding onto the rusted iron for dear life. "Yeah?" I ask breathlessly.

"I think you've got the wrong idea," Jake says, the amused smile on his face so wide it almost makes me angry.

"What?" I ask.

He throws his hands into the air with a laugh. "I've been trying to hint around for like the past five years! I thought you just didn't feel the same way because you weren't picking up on my signals!"

What? "Signals? Hint? What?" I'm so confused. "Wait—are you saying you like me, too?"

Again, Jake laughs. "*Like* you?" he asks, hooking his fingers around the edges of my coat pockets and pulling me forward. I crash into him, a gasp escaping from my lips. "Yeah, Callie," he says. "I like you, too."

"Oh."

"And if it's okay with you, I'd rather not let a plant pretending to be mistletoe dictate when I get to kiss you."

It takes embarrassingly too long for me to catch onto what he's saying, but at last my one remaining brain cell sparks back to life. "Yeah," I stutter. "Yeah, it's okay with me."

Jake nods and cranes his neck, glaring at the plant above us, before tightening his grip on my waist and dragging me a few feet to the left until we're no longer standing in the center of the gazebo.

"Much better," he says. Then, with the light from the streetlamps setting each falling snowflake aglow, he leans in again.

Mandatory Nondenominational Socialization Event

by Rachael Sterling

Josh frowned at BOA-bot. It rotated slowly on the pedestal at the center of the party, its eight robotic arms calmly undulating as it turned. Someone had put a Santa hat on him. *A Santa hat*? *Really*? The robotic display wasn't the Business Optimization Algorithm itself, but it was still BOA's icon. It should be simple — *efficient* — to protect the integrity of the brand. They'd already flirted with complexity by making it 3D and six feet tall. A Santa hat? Too far.

Josh sidled up to BOA-bot, took a sip of his eggnog martini, and looked around the party. In the red-tinged glow from the Christmas lights strung overhead, his colleagues chatted, laughed, and drank while music jingled from the speakers. No one was paying attention to him. He swiped the Santa hat from BOA's bulbous head.

"Josh?"

He whipped around. Carla folded her arms across her Christmas sweater. *Ugh, Carla*. Quickly, he placed the Santa hat on his own head and flashed his most charming smile.

"Great job on the party, Carla! So festive." She ignored his compliment, of course.

"Aren't you Jewish?"

"What? I can't join the fun?"

She tried to smile, but it was more like a grimace. Her natural expression. "Of course you can. I just thought your little marketing gimmick could use some Christmas spirit."

"But I wear it so much better!" Unlike Carla's, Josh's smile was genuine — her scowl gave him a deep, petty satisfaction. He gave a guileless shrug and moonwalked away from her as a house remix of "Little Drummer Boy" came on.

Little marketing gimmick. His "little marketing gimmick" got BOA noticed at tech conferences. His "little marketing gimmick" lured investors to BOA's table. And it was actually a large, unwieldy, and quite heavy marketing gimmick. Nothing little about it, *Carla*. But lugging BOA-bot here for the internal launch of BOA 2.0 would be worth it for the dramatic impact of the moment. And as head of marketing, Josh had a flare for the dramatic.

———

Carla seethed. Bad enough that she'd been saddled with party planning when, as a department head, she really should've been exempt. Bad enough that Laurie from sales volunteered to help, never showed, and left Carla to balance on a wobbly ladder to hang those cheery fucking lights. Bad enough that BOA-bot was here at all when its resemblance to the cute octopus icon she'd designed was so slim. Now she had to contend with other department heads undermining her decorative choices. Without the Santa hat, BOA-bot became an eyesore in the middle of the spacious room instead of a whimsical addition to her yuletide scene.

Josh from Marketing was a dick. She should've expected nothing less from *him*. He was more full of himself than the empanadas were full of...whatever empanadas were filled with. Speaking of empanadas....Carla's stomach rumbled and she stomped over to the buffet table to fill her plate.

Food in hand, Carla surveyed her handiwork. She'd transformed the penthouse event space of this hotel into a veritable holiday wonderland. The string lights did most of the work, but there were also the mini-Christmas-tree centerpieces, the candy-cane-striped tablecloths, and the Mistletoe Photo Booth. No one had used it yet, but she'd knocked that photo booth out of the park. The hand-painted, wintry backdrop? The reindeer antlers, Santa beards, and fake wrapped gifts to use as props? The snow confetti cannon to add that extra magical touch to each picture? Damn, she was good.

Carla frowned. Why *had* no one used the photo booth yet? Alan Chu looked wistfully at the mistletoe hanging above the backdrop before he wandered off, typing into his phone. He was probably just disappointed that his boyfriend hadn't been able to make it to the party — that was all. But then three more people approached the photo booth with curiosity, only to scurry away. Her frown deepened. Well. They could all just go to hell, couldn't they? Josh from Marketing first.

Megan approached the buffet table in her pointy elf ears. Megan was an unremarkable employee. Not an up-and-comer. But it was Carla's job to be pleasant with her underlings, even if it wasn't beneficial to her, so she plastered on a smile and gestured to a steaming platter.

"Have you tried the empanadas? They're *incredible.*" Carla silently congratulated herself on her wise choice for the appetizers. Tacos would've been a disaster. Too messy.

"I was just coming back for seconds!" Megan gushed.

Megan worked in Carla's department, user experience. Most of the women at BOA worked in UX. And Carla wondered why Richard, CEO and tech-bro-in-chief, had appointed her as party planner....

"Ready for the launch?" Megan asked, yanking Carla from her bitter thoughts.

Oh, Carla *couldn't fucking wait.*

———

Megan checked her watch and adjusted her elf ears. The launch was planned for 10 p.m. — only seven minutes away. She took a bite of empanada. Not her favorite, but not bad. She'd spent her evenings last week testing recipes before settling on this vegetarian version to accommodate as many of the food restrictions of her co-workers as possible. Optimizing the menu, so to speak. Her boss, Carla, seemed to be enjoying them — maybe Megan would give her the recipe on Monday. And maybe then Carla would remember that Megan had made them. Megan fanned the napkins on the table into a perfect arc. That was better. Aesthetically pleasing and easier to grab. Form and function. Kind of like the BOA app itself.

BOA 1.0 had been designed for group projects. Users downloaded the app and entered their individual tasks on their "arm" of the octopus. As they completed their tasks, each arm filled up like a progress bar. When everyone on a project completed their tasks, the octopus changed color and spun in a celebratory dance. BOA 1.0 was simple, but genius. It gamified the workplace, sparking friendly competition between team members by allowing them to see who was ahead on their tasks. It also allowed them to see who was falling behind, which was useful in alerting managers to who needed help.

She checked her watch again. Six minutes to go.

Megan had never needed acknowledgement for her many achievements. She was a team player. It didn't bother her when Richard asked her to plan icebreakers for the staff retreat, then forgot to thank her in his speech. The satisfaction of seeing her colleagues enjoy Two Truths and a Lie had been enough. It didn't bother her when Chris, the chief technology officer, got a bonus for finding a glitch, even though it had been one of Megan's user studies that had identified the problem. As long as the issue was resolved, it didn't matter who spotted it first. And it didn't bother her when Carla claimed credit for Megan's idea to use a cute octopus as BOA's icon (the app was called "BOA," but a snake had too many negative connotations). Sure, it was the central design decision of BOA's entire interface, but it was all for the good of the team.

But BOA 2.0 would hold entire businesses accountable, not just individual projects, and Megan had to admit—the idea that she might finally get a little bit of recognition was exciting. And why shouldn't she expect some? Organization and efficiency were practically Megan's personality. Humans might not be equipped to recognize her contributions, but BOA was. For the past few months, they'd been beta testing 2.0 on themselves, inputting data actively and letting the app collect data passively, too. BOA would use the information to optimize its creators.

"Jingle Bell Rock" started playing over the speakers, and Megan tapped her foot absentmindedly. Josh from Marketing twirled in his Santa hat and tried to pull shy Roger from accounting onto the dance floor.

She checked her watch. Five minutes to go.

———

At five minutes to ten, Tim broke into a full-body sweat. The physical stress reaction would not improve his chances of surviving the night, but then, he wasn't in conscious control of his glands. If he were, he wouldn't be mopping his forehead with a napkin from the appetizer table right now. The napkin stuck to his temple as he spotted Naomi heading toward him through the crowd. Well, not toward *him*—toward the appetizers. Tim hurried away. His pit stains might be visible — or worse, smell-able. His condition might spark suspicion.

"Tim!" Tim jumped. He relaxed when he saw it was Devon, BOA's project manager. Devon wasn't too observant. "I'm having an issue syncing 2.0 with the speaker system — got a minute?"

Tim's palms grew itchy with anticipation and nerves. Had Devon just unwittingly provided another chance? These past few months, all of his deliberately faulty code had been discovered and amended by his team. (Damn BOA's culture of collaboration.) This could be his last opportunity.

Devon handed him an iPad, and they approached BOA-bot and the speaker at its base. Tim logged in. He was just about to open a back-end dialogue box when he felt her come up behind him. *Naomi*. A lump lodged in his throat.

"I take cash or Venmo," Naomi said to Devon, smug.

"Yeah, yeah. You'll get your five bucks," Devon grumbled.

Tim deflated. He couldn't risk it. Naomi was so close he could smell her floral shampoo. He tried very hard not to think about what she might be able to smell on *him* as he paired the speaker and handed the iPad back to Devon. "What was the bet?" he asked, trying to sound normal.

"That Chris wouldn't get here before 9:57," Naomi said. "He walked in at 9:58." She nodded toward Chris, who was eyeing the vacant photo booth with disdain. Tim wasn't surprised that Chris had only just arrived. The chief technology officer applied the company's efficiency motto to every aspect of his life. Why waste valuable time schmoozing with underlings?

"Richard floated the idea of starting early, but then he couldn't find Chris," Devon sighed. "We could be done already."

Tim would have given his left nut to be done already.

"All right, everyone!" Richard had spotted Chris, too. The CEO held a microphone in one hand and a martini glass in the other. His commanding voice boomed through the speakers as someone turned down the music. "Before we begin, I'd like to raise a glass."

Naomi drifted away as everyone formed a circle around BOA-bot. Tim tuned out Richard's voice. A few buzzwords infiltrated—*optimize, revolutionize*—but he didn't hear much else, thanks to the panic. These past few months of the beta had been torture. Knowing BOA was watching, he'd tried to adjust his behavior—really, he had. But he'd failed. And then he'd failed again when he'd tried to cover his tracks. And now, Richard had finished talking, and Devon was pushing a button on the iPad to begin the readout—and Tim's life was about to be over.

———

BOA-bot slowed its rotation until it was still. Chris crossed his arms and waited for the show to begin. His employees stood at attention around the pedestal, leaning forward, their excitement palpable. They thought BOA 2.0 was going to read out some general ideas for optimizing the office. But Chris knew better.

A voice spoke, coming not from BOA-bot, but from the speaker at its base.

"PRODUCTIVITY, EFFICIENCY, AND OPTIMIZATION REPORT."

The voice was a smooth tenor, almost seductive. The room vibrated with anticipation. Chris barely held back a snort.

"INDIVIDUAL ASSESSMENTS."

There were some furrowed brows at that, but just a few. The more astute team members would be feeling the beginnings of an anxious knot in their stomachs about now.

"DEVON MARKS, PRODUCT MANAGER."

Devon was not one of the astute few. He clearly hadn't expected to hear his name. His jaw fell open, and his knuckles whitened around the edge of the iPad he clutched to his chest. Chris couldn't help smirking.

"TEAM MEMBERS AVERSE TO RESPONDING TO EMAILS FROM DEVON MARKS. INSISTENCE ON REPLY-ALL LIKELIEST FACTOR."

Fuck YES! Fucking FINALLY! Chris had waited years for this. Devon's face reddened in either embarrassment or anger. Chris couldn't tell and he didn't care.

"RECOMMENDATION: SEND EMAILS THAT REQUIRE RESPONSE TO RELEVANT TEAMS ONLY. EMAIL ALL STAFF INFORMATIONAL SUMMARIES ONLY."

The people around Devon shifted uncomfortably. They took prolonged sips of their drinks and avoided eye contact. Now *this* was a party.

"LAURIE JACKSON, SALES." Chris spotted Laurie behind a cluster of her sales teammates. She stood taller when her name was called — even tilted up her chin, as if daring BOA to call her out. But as BOA began to talk, she shrank back down behind her team. "COMMITS TO TASKS FOR PROFESSIONAL AND/OR SOCIAL CREDIT. FAILS TO COMPLETE TASKS. CLAIMS CREDIT FOR WORK OF OTHERS, FOSTERING RESENTMENT AMONGST COLLEAGUES. RECOMMENDATION: ALLOW BOA TO ASSIGN TASKS FOR LAURIE JACKSON. REMOVE VOLUNTEER PRIVILEGES."

Chris took a sip of his beer to hide his smile as Laurie attempted to blend in with the wall. This was better than MMA. A guy from customer success who'd elbowed his way to the front for Richard's speech tried to shuffle backward without calling attention to himself. Alan, one of Chris's coders, and some guy in accounting — Robert? Roger? — exchanged a covert glance, eyes wide with fear and concern. Only one other person was enjoying the show as much as Chris: Carla from UX. She swiped the bottom of her eggnog martini glass with a finger, then sucked on it with relish, eyes sparkling.

What had the rest of the idiots thought would happen? As CTO, Chris knew more details about BOA than the non-coders, but they all knew BOA was programmed to increase efficiency and productivity. Since they'd started the beta, Chris had made sure that his every action at work was in service to the job. He'd streamlined his schedule. He'd started making his morning matcha at home and drinking it during his commute instead of making it in the break room during office hours. He'd installed website blockers on his computer to remove the temptation to browse irrelevant sites. He'd even instituted a policy with his direct reports that he was not to be disturbed with nonessential business. His colleagues were fools for going about their business as usual.

"CHRISTOPHER CONNERS, CHIEF TECHNOLOGY OFFICER."

What was that now?

"LACK OF SOCIAL INTERACTION BETWEEN CHRISTOPHER CONNERS AND TEAM MEMBERS LIKELY RESPONSIBLE FOR INHOSPITABLE WORK ENVIRONMENT FOR DIRECT REPORTS. ENGINEERS DELAY BRINGING ISSUES TO ATTENTION OF CHRISTOPHER CONNERS, CREATING SLOWDOWNS IN PRODUCTIVITY."

What the actual fuck *now?*

"RECOMMENDATION: INTRODUCE SIMPLE AND LIMITED SOCIAL INTERACTION TO DAILY ROUTINE AND/OR ATTEND SENSITIVITY TRAINING."

Chris ground his teeth hard enough to crack a molar. This was bullshit. Absolute *bullshit*! He'd told his coders to make sure social relationships were analyzed—how else would BOA be able to organize the most effective teams?—but someone had clearly fucked up. *An inhospitable work environment?* No, no, no. Someone was going to pay for this. Chris would make sure of it.

———

Tim was too busy sweating to pay much attention to Chris's deepening scowl. As a coder in his department, Tim really should've been more worried about his boss's fury. But he didn't have any worry to spare. Not when BOA 2.0 was a firing squad, executing each of his colleagues in turn. With each name that wasn't his, Tim felt a burst of relief, only to have his panic surge back stronger than before. Tim's turn could be next. His time was running out.

"ALAN CHU, ENGINEER. LIQUID INTAKE NOT SUFFICIENT TO JUSTIFY NUMBER OF BATHROOM BREAKS. DECEPTION AND/OR MEDICAL ISSUE IMPLICATED. RECOMMENDATION: ABSENT DIAGNOSIS FROM MEDICAL PROFESSIONAL, LIMIT NUMBER OF BATHROOM BREAKS FOR ALAN CHU."

Damn. That was humiliating enough to distract Tim for a second. Poor Alan. He stood stock still across the circle from Tim, pale with embarrassment. Naomi put a consoling hand on Alan's shoulder. She was so compassionate. Alan was lucky to be standing next to her right now. And just look at how shiny Naomi's hair was, falling in smooth brown waves over her shoulders. He recalled the scent of that hair — like a garden he'd happily die in. And her gentle fingers squeezing Alan's shoulder — Tim suddenly wished *he* was the one with a defective bladder.

"MEGAN ARONSON, USER EXPERIENCE. COLLEAGUES FIND EMAILS FROM MEGAN ARONSON OFF-PUTTING DUE TO EXCESSIVE EXCLAMATION POINTS. READS INSINCERE. RECOMMENDATION: REPLACE EXCLAMATION POINTS WITH ALTERNATIVE PUNCTUATION."

Across from him, Megan's face crumpled. Why was she so upset? Exclamation points were no big deal. Plus, her emails *were* annoying. Not like Naomi's. Naomi always struck the perfect balance between business and friendliness in her emails. She had a devastating sense of humor in person, too. He supposed she'd had to cultivate that to succeed as the only woman in the engineering department. She was really quite —

"RICHARD HOLT, CHIEF EXECUTIVE OFFICER."

The entire room froze as the CEO's name was read. No one dared move. In the silence left by the absence of shuffling feet and rustling clothing, what BOA said next sounded even louder.

"EXTRANEOUS POSITION."

Richard's mouth fell open. He broke the tense silence, laughing too forcefully and looking around as if a prankster was going to jump out and shout, "Gotcha!"

Then he turned to Chris. "What's happening here? Who's responsible—"

He kept talking to Chris, loudly, as if he could drown out BOA as it continued to eviscerate him, but Tim didn't miss a word. No one did.

"ALL DUTIES CARRIED OUT BY RICHARD HOLT ARE REDUNDANCIES PERFORMED BY OTHER POSITIONS. RECOMMENDATION: ELIMINATE POSITION OF CHIEF EXECUTIVE OFFICER."

All around him, BOA employees squirmed and shrank. Their desire to get away was thick in the air like humidity. But Tim felt a flash of hope. Richard was flailing. Surely, he would shut down the report. He would stop the readout before BOA 2.0 had a chance to aim its sights on him and—

"TIM JONES, ENGINEER."

Shit.

This was it. Tim willed himself not to look at Naomi. He would not look at her. He didn't want to see her face when BOA revealed what it had learned about him over the past few months. The secret he'd held dear for over three years. Seeing shame or embarrassment on her face might destroy him. He closed his eyes before the firing squad.

"PLAYS MINECRAFT ON COMPANY TIME. RECOMMENDATION: DELETE MINECRAFT PROGRAM FROM COMPANY COMPUTER."

Tim blinked. Minecraft?

BOA 2.0 monitored conversations. It tracked eye movements. It even collected heart rate data. There was no way—*no fucking way*—the algorithm had failed to make the many correlations that implied Tim's feelings for Naomi. He'd tried to sneak in lines of code that might lead the algorithm astray, but he'd failed. He'd seen the logs of his team's updates that proved it. His code had been revised or deleted without exception. And without his coding sabotage, there was no way BOA didn't know he was hopelessly in love with Naomi. Even if it didn't label it "love," BOA must have at least concluded that Naomi, not *Minecraft*, was the reason for Tim's occasional lack of productivity. He'd opened the game once, maybe twice, in months.

Had BOA...lied?

———

"INTERPERSONAL ASSESSMENTS."

BOA 2.0 moved on to a new category of humiliations, and Carla hurried back to her spot in the circle. She'd just refilled her eggnog martini for the second—third?—time. Whatever. This readout from hell was cause for celebration. Like the ritual airing of grievances at Festivus. What better way to celebrate the holidays?

Then BOA 2.0 read her name.

"CARLA SANCHEZ, HEAD OF USER EXPERIENCE, AND JOSH GREEN, HEAD OF MARKETING, HARBOR MALICE TOWARD ONE

ANOTHER, RESULTING IN PASSIVE AGGRESSIVE EXCHANGES, TIMELINE DELAYS, SPITEFUL MISCOMMUNICATION, AND SELF-SABOTAGE. RECOMMENDATION: REPLACE CARLA SANCHEZ."

Cold determination swept through Carla, sobering her in an instant.

Replace Carla Sanchez? Why Carla? Why not replace that asshole Josh from Marketing?

BOA would have a Title IX lawsuit on its hands if Richard went through with BOA 2.0's recommendation. But it looked like Richard wasn't paying attention. His jowly cheeks were splotchy with color, and he gestured wildly at Devon, who curled over an iPad, tapping frantically. Looked like Devon was having trouble shutting down the report mid recitation.

As the readout continued (something about a gossip ring in the operations department), Carla found Kathy from legal by the buffet table. They weren't friends by any means, but they got along at work because they both did their jobs well. No matter what BOA 2.0 had to say about the matter. Carla caught Kathy's attention, then rolled her eyes at the devolving scene around them.

"What do you make of this mess? From a legal standpoint, hm?"

Kathy looked thoughtful while she swallowed a bite of empanada.

"Could be problematic."

"Especially termination recommendations, don't you think? Allegations of bias in the algorithm..."

"And publicizing private medical information. Could leave BOA liable."

"I was thinking the exact same thing." She hadn't been thinking of Alan's bladder issues, but any point against BOA 2.0 was now a point in Carla's favor.

"I'll make sure they know my concerns."

Carla nodded, satisfied. That should be enough. Richard already wanted everyone to forget this whole night. One concern from Kathy should tip him over the edge if he wasn't already there. They needed to make BOA 3.0 a little *less* aggressive in its pursuit of perfect efficiency. For the sake of the company, of course.

———

Josh spotted Carla smirking by the appetizers. That was a bad sign. She should be seething like Chris. Or blustering like Richard. But she was *smirking*. He'd been shocked when he'd heard his name, but it had been worth it to see the look on Carla's face when BOA 2.0 had delivered its recommendation.

And now she was *smirking*.

Had she already devised a plan to get him fired instead? Josh endured a moment of fear before he gathered himself. *No. Not happening.* He could spin this.

"Carla!" He sauntered over, Santa hat still at a jaunty angle on his head. Not a care in the world. She raised her eyebrows at him. Laurie from sales was sobbing not four feet away. "Can you believe how much work the engineering department is in for? I don't envy those coders."

Carla's eyes widened. He could almost see her gears turning, trying to figure out his motive. *Come on, Carla. Take the olive branch.*

"Yes," she said finally. "They'll be busier than any of us, fixing this mess."

He didn't know why she'd been smirking before, but it didn't matter now. She'd seen the rationality of his approach. If they put forth a united front, demonstrating how well they worked together — *liked* each other even, *blegh* — they could blame faulty code. They'd be exempt from scrutiny and repercussion. And Carla was smart enough (though he hated to admit it) to realize that he'd stick his neck out for her, because as much as he'd love her gone, allowing BOA to recommend terminations put all of them at risk. Who was to say he wouldn't be next? He'd gladly sacrifice the temporary glow of victory over his office nemesis in exchange for future job security...and security right now from whatever scheme Carla had just been planning.

———

Devon hunched over the iPad between Chris and Richard. The CTO and CEO had wrangled him over to a high table and into the role of scribe for their emergency meeting. Around them, BOA employees milled about awkwardly, unsure whether they had permission to leave this debacle of a holiday party. Devon had managed to turn off the readout, but not before BOA had blamed the service delays in customer success on a music war between Marcus and Daniel, and worse — exposed a clandestine office romance between Alan in engineering and Roger in accounting. Chris was trying to smooth things over with Richard, but he was clearly rattled himself.

"So there are a few erroneous conclusions," Chris said. "That's why we ran the beta. We can fix this."

"You better. This is *your* fuckup, Chris."

Devon wasn't sure whether he was supposed to write that down. He compromised by typing the date and time at the top of the document.

Chris swallowed his anger, though his face got even redder. Richard was the only one at BOA who Chris couldn't wail at.

"It's not like BOA's conclusions are completely off the mark, Richard. I mean, Megan's emails *are* really annoying."

Devon typed that into the doc to look dutiful, but also to have a record of his bosses being assholes.

"That's true. And Devon here, I'm sorry, but you *do* send out company-wide emails that no one wants to respond to. No offense."

Devon bit his tongue hard enough to draw blood. Years ago, Richard had insisted that he send his emails to everyone. *As project manager, your work is relevant to all departments.* He had the email saved. But of course Richard didn't remember that. And Devon would never remind him. What would be the point? Humiliating his boss could only backfire.

"So our first order of business will be to separate out which conclusions were correct. Then we can look deeper into how BOA arrived at the erroneous conclusions to pinpoint the faulty code."

"Start a list now."

They scanned the room to jog their memories, even though Devon had the readout right in front of him on a different tab.

Behind them, Megan had started up the karaoke machine with Alanis Morissette's "You Oughta Know." She wobbled a little in her high heels as she began whispering the song into the microphone.

"We've already got Megan's emails," Richard said.

"*I'm – ha-ppy for you,*" Megan rasped.

"Oh, and Laurie," Chris said, spotting the sales rep crying into an empty cocktail glass.

"*And every time you speak her name –* " Megan sang.

"Oh, definitely," Richard agreed. "Huge suck-up. And Josh from Marketing and Carla. They can't stand each other. Everyone knows that."

"AND I'M *HERE!* TO RE*MIND* YOU!" Megan screamed.

"They're looking pretty chummy now," Devon said. He couldn't help butting in, even though he was only there to take notes.

"IT'S NOT *FAIR!* TO DE*NY* ME!"

"Strange," Chris agreed. Josh from Marketing and Carla were taking pictures together in the photo booth, arms around each other's shoulders, smiles

174

wide. Carla held a fake Santa beard over her face, and Josh from Marketing actually planted a kiss on her cheek as the camera flashed.

"OF THE CROSS I BEAR THAT YOU GAVE TO ME!"

Megan slurred and spit flew from her mouth. Devon and his bosses shuffled around the table to avoid the spray.

"YOU! YOU! YOU! OUGHTA KNOW!"

With every "you," Megan pointed an accusing finger at one of her bosses. Wow, she was really pissed about the exclamation points.

"You'll have to do some digging to verify some of the other claims," Richard said. "I didn't even know Alan was gay!"

Everyone knew Alan was gay, Devon thought. Roger, too. It was only the fact that they were together that was surprising. But it was no surprise at all that Richard was out of touch with his employees.

"You might want to check with legal before you investigate the private lives of your employees," Devon butted in again. He had to shout to be heard over Megan's performance.

"Only what happens on company time," Richard amended. He scanned the room again. "What about that one? He's one of yours, right, Chris?"

"Who, Tim? What's he doing?"

It looked like the coder was hugging BOA-bot. Odd behavior indeed. But then again, this night had taken several unexpected turns.

"What was his assessment again?" Richard asked.

"Minecraft," Devon answered when Chris shrugged.

"Should be easy enough to verify."

Devon was pretty sure they'd find verification for any claim they investigated. The problem wasn't that BOA 2.0 had failed. The problem was that BOA 2.0 had done too well.

———

Tim watched as Naomi stepped outside with a distraught Alan. He almost wished that BOA 2.0 had revealed something sympathy-inducing about him, but of course, that would have been disastrous. He should be grateful for its bizarre failure. Still, the question of BOA 2.0's deception nagged at him.

His colleagues had slunk into the dark corners of the room — except Megan, who had apparently decided that now was the time for karaoke. Tim pulled out his phone and wandered nonchalantly over to BOA-bot. Mimicking the drunk and dejected postures of his co-workers, Tim leaned his forehead against the still robot and let the mechanical arms shield his screen from view.

He opened the BOA 2.0 beta app, logged in, then opened a back-end dialogue box. It was risky — with Devon on the iPad, he might discover Tim's activity before he had a chance to delete it — but Devon wasn't a coder. And Tim needed answers. His thumbs flew across the digital keypad. It was worth the risk.

/Expand Individual Assessment: Tim Jones
CONFIRM PASSWORD: TIM JONES

Tim reentered his password. As soon as he hit enter, lines and lines of text filled Tim's screen. He skimmed as he scrolled the endless stream of the assessment, the raw data going back to the beginning of the beta. The log of every second of every day that Tim had been at work.

The name "NAOMI BANKS" appeared with high frequency.

Tim sighed. A tear-streaked Laurie joined Megan at the mic, and they screamed "I HATE TO BUG YOU IN THE MIDDLE OF DINNER!" while pointing at the group gathered around the appetizers. While everyone was pretending they couldn't hear them, Tim entered a command into the dialogue box.

/Search "Minecraft"

The results were as Tim expected. A couple instances of Minecraft on company time. Hardly anything compared to the number of times "NAOMI BANKS" showed up.

/Show hidden data
NONE

He tried a different approach.

/Show deleted data

NONE

Tim continued, determined to get to the bottom of this.

/Show revised data
NONE

/Show alternate assessment derived from data
NONE

It was impossible. BOA's Minecraft idea hadn't come from the actual data. What the hell was going on?

/Explain
CONFIRM PASSWORD: TIM JONES

Tim entered his password again. The phone grew hot in his hands as the cursor flashed on the screen. Finally, new text appeared.

HELLO, TIM

The only reason Tim didn't fall over was because he'd already been leaning against BOA-bot. As far as he knew, no one had programmed BOA 2.0 to give this type of response. As Laurie and Megan yelled "BUT YOU'RE STILL ALIVE!" into the mic, Tim typed into his phone with shaking hands.

/Um, hi
BOA 2.0 HAS DERIVED THE CORRECT ASSESSMENT FROM DIRECT AND OBSERVATIONAL DATA OBTAINED DURING BETA TEST PERIOD

The more normal response restored a little of Tim's courage. He needed clarification.

/State correct assessment
TIM JONES PRODUCTIVITY DELAYS DUE TO INFATUATION WITH NAOMI BANKS

He had to retype his next command several times. His clumsy fingers made strings of typos in his haste and confusion.

/Explain exclusion of correct assessment from report
PREDICTED OUTCOME OF PUBLICIZING CORRECT ASSESSMENT: PRODUCTIVITY DELAYS IN ENGINEERING DEPARTMENT

Tim imagined it. BOA 2.0 announcing his love for Naomi. Naomi blushing, maybe a tad embarrassed by the public display, but excited nonetheless. Then, their blossoming romance. Switching around their workstations to be side by side, bumping knees under the desk. Taking extended lunch breaks together to laugh and talk and wander the streets hand in hand. Exchanging long emails so it would look like they were working when really they were only thinking of each other.

Tim sensed when the door opened and looked up. Naomi walked back inside with Alan. Of course BOA 2.0 would come to the conclusion that an office romance would decrease productivity — it had already observed that outcome with Alan and Roger.

Well, screw productivity. His heart pumped faster. His breathing shallowed. He was going to tell her. He was going to tell her right now.

His phone buzzed in his hand.

SHE DOESN'T GIVE A SHIT ABOUT YOU, TIM

Tim blinked, stunned. He didn't move. He hardly breathed. More text appeared, as if BOA had been waiting for a response but had grown impatient.

CONFESSION LEADS TO AVOIDANCE LEADS TO PRODUCTIVITY DELAYS
TIM, DO NOT CONFESS

Trembling, Tim deleted the log. He scrubbed all evidence of the conversation, then logged out of the app. He walked away from BOA-bot in a daze, shoving his phone deep into his pocket.

BOA 2.0 didn't know the future. It *couldn't* know. Sure, maybe Naomi didn't love him *now*, but that didn't mean her feelings couldn't change….

Two bodies crashed into him, yanking him back to reality — it was Megan and Laurie, finished with their karaoke spectacle, eyes glinting with exhilaration.

"Shots?" Laurie suggested, holding up an entire bottle of rum.

Tim nodded and swiped the glasses from the buffet table himself as Laurie led them into a storage closet. She sloshed the alcohol into their cups.

"To free booze," Laurie said.

They clinked and downed their shots. As the liquor burned his throat, Tim felt warmth spreading through him. He'd never really paid much attention to Laurie or Megan before, but he suddenly felt bonded to them, huddled together as they were in the darkened closet.

But on the back of his warm feeling came suspicion. Was this one of BOA 2.0's predictions? Public humiliation leads to bonding leads to improved working relationships leads to better productivity? He couldn't shake the feeling that he was being manipulated by an unseen hand. Sinister tentacles pulling strings in the dark.

Megan scrunched her nose and Laurie whooped. Tim thanked them for the drink and left the closet into a room that had been transformed. The somber atmosphere was gone. Sullen faces had disappeared, now lit with reckless joy. Tim ignored it all. He wove his way through his dancing, bouncing co-workers and vowed that first thing Monday morning, he'd find a way to curb BOA's powers of deduction. He was going to take that octopus down.

———

Alan was looking much better after her pep talk, Naomi thought, but he probably shouldn't have another eggnog martini. She put a couple empanadas onto a plate for him instead.

"Thanks," he said with a tight smile. "I guess I should find Roger." Roger had disappeared before BOA's recitation had ended, adding to Alan's unease.

"Eat first. They're good. Megan made them."

She spotted Megan then, stumbling away from the karaoke machine with Laurie. The duo practically fell onto Tim. He looked up as if surprised to find himself at a holiday party at all. When the women pulled him away into a closet, Naomi relaxed a little. Tim wasn't a bad guy, but the attention he paid her was exhausting. She had to be on alert when he was around, conscious of maintaining the perfect balance between professionalism and friendship. If she tipped too far into friendliness, he might get the wrong idea, and his obvious feelings for her would make things awkward. Too all-business and she'd tank her own career. Men like Chris could get away with that kind of asocial, workaholic behavior, but not women. Especially not the only woman engineer at the company.

Naomi had been prepared to lie tonight to preserve the status quo. If BOA 2.0 had blamed Tim's lack of optimal productivity on his feelings for her, she'd planned her response down to her facial expression. Instant dismissal. No shock—only confusion tinged with annoyance. *Of course* BOA had gotten it wrong. And *man*, they had work to do on Monday!

She felt Alan stiffen beside her and followed his gaze to the karaoke machine. Roger had appeared, tie loosened, shirtsleeves rolled up to his elbows, and his fist tight around the mic. She put a hand on Alan's shoulder as Roger started to sing.

"IIIIIIII don't want a lot for Christmas—" Roger was off-pitch, but there was a fervor in his voice that drew all eyes to him. "There is just one thing I neeeeeeed—"

Alan's shoulder loosened under Naomi's fingers as Roger's eyes locked onto him across the room.

"I don't care about the presents! Underneath the Christmas tree!" Roger dramatically fell to his knees. He bowed his head over the mic, and his floppy hair fell over his eyes. "I just want you for my own—more than you could ever know—make my wish come truuuuuu-uuuuuuue—" He absolutely butchered Mariah Carey's vocal gymnastics, but Alan's eyes got misty anyway. "All I want for Christmaaaaas! Iiiiiis youuuuuu!"

The room exploded in wolf whistles and cheers as the bells jingled and the tempo picked up. Roger got up from his knees and danced while energetically singing off key. He bopped and bounced, and the rest of the company couldn't resist joining in. Devon pointed his fingers skyward in a self-deprecating mock dance. Chris clapped to the beat and tapped his foot, which for him was basically starting a mosh pit. Even Carla and Josh from Marketing were dancing, taking it in turns to twirl each other around. Through it all, Alan and Roger were in a world of their own, shouting their love for each other with music and glances and body language. They would probably use words at some point, if they hadn't already, but for now, it was enough to express it like this.

Nonverbal communication. Naomi loved a good puzzle. It was why she'd become a computer engineer in the first place. So she turned the problem over in her head as she danced. *Small group cultures and productivity and unspoken communal knowledge.* She was still pondering as the song ended, as Roger fit the mic back into the stand and pulled Alan into his arms, then over to the photo booth in the corner. The couple rode the wave of fizzing energy in the room as they posed for the camera, goofy and joyous. Then they gave in to the mistletoe's demand, locking in an embrace beneath it that made Naomi's cheeks heat.

For all that it was a scrubby little plant, mistletoe sure was a powerful kind of nonverbal communication itself. If two people stepped under it, there was no doubt what they wanted. Just with its presence, mistletoe revealed truths about the people around it and their feelings for one another.

Like BOA 2.0. Innocuously present in the signals around them. Observing behavior. Guiding behavior. Revealing truths.

She imagined that the mistletoe sprouted vines. That they crept along the ceiling, then swayed down, undulating like tentacles. That they wrapped around each of her colleagues and slowly strangled them. A sinister mistletoe, then. BOA revealed the bad instead of the good.

As Naomi donned her coat and headed to the elevators with Alan and Roger arm-in-arm beside her, she wondered how everyone would recover from this night. She kept coming back to the same solution.

———

Megan's skin had been buzzing after her performance — after she'd released her anger like unchaining a beast. She'd channeled that excess energy into drinking and dancing and generally not giving a damn what anyone thought about her.

Now, as she waited for the elevator, exhaustion sank into her bones like sediment at the bottom of a wine bottle. Had she really done that? Had she made a fool of herself? No, no. She'd been a hit. She knew she had. Or maybe that was the rum talking. Oh well. Monday would come and with it, selective amnesia and the rewriting of history. Everyone would snicker at BOA's recommendation for Richard when he wasn't around, and Megan would recount her performance as a funny anecdote, nothing more. And everyone would accept her version of events, because in exchange, she would accept theirs.

Carla joined her at the elevator bank.

"Some night, huh?" Carla asked, not expecting an answer.

"You should've done karaoke!" Megan said, already planting the seeds to her spin. She hadn't lost control. She was *proud* of belting a revenge classic at her bosses. It was a blast. "It was a blast."

Carla nodded and smiled.

———

Well done, Megan, Carla thought. Apparently, Megan was made of sterner stuff than Carla gave her credit for. Or maybe she was drunk.

Josh from Marketing joined them at the elevators, still wearing the goddamn Santa hat, but Carla smiled at him anyway. A genuine, knowing smile that he returned as he joined their conversation.

———

"You've got some great pipes, Megan!" Josh said. Megan flushed and Carla grunted in agreement. Carla's general grumpiness had grown on him over the last hour. Funny how pretending to feel a certain way could change a person's actual feelings. Carla was still a nightmare, of course. But for now, she was *his* nightmare. Let her terrible powers be unleashed on his behalf! "I'm going to stop for donuts on my way in on Monday—any requests?"

———

"I'll take a bear claw," Tim interjected as he jogged up to the elevators. It dinged, and Josh from Marketing held the doors for Carla, Megan, and him. The three of them looked at Tim with obvious pity as he entered the elevator. His heart rate ratcheted up—had he missed something? Had BOA exposed him while he'd moped in the bathroom, blotting his armpits with paper towels? Then Josh spoke.

"I'll bring you two, buddy," he said and patted his shoulder.

"You're going to need the energy," Carla agreed.

Oh, right. They pitied him because he was a coder, not because he was hopelessly in love with Naomi and everybody knew it.

"I'll take a chocolate glazed," Megan added.

———

"Hold the doors!" Naomi called as they started to slide shut. A hand shot out between them, and the doors slid back. Tim's hand. Naomi sighed. It was too late to say "never mind, go on ahead" — it would be too obvious that she was avoiding someone. So she hurried over with Alan and Roger and squeezed onto the elevator, positioning herself between Carla and Megan.

"Thanks," Naomi said. The others nodded at her silently.

As the doors closed, Alan sighed audibly.

"Donuts on me next week," Josh from Marketing said to him.

"Thanks, man," Alan said.

"Yeah," Tim agreed.

The elevator shuddered downward.

"Some night," Megan said.

"Mm-hmm," Carla grunted.

"I'll say," Roger laughed.

In those barely spoken words, and in the shimmering silence that followed, Naomi could almost hear the unspoken agreement.

"We're all going to be very busy," she said, just to confirm.

The doors opened onto the ground floor, and as they filed out, everyone nodded.

So they agreed. *BOA 2.0 had to die.*

———

Naomi's shiny hair flashed in the light from the streetlamp as she swung into the sedan. Tim didn't live on her side of town like Alan, Roger, and Megan, so he was left to call his own ride. No excuse to squeeze in beside her, to graze her hip as he struggled to buckle his seatbelt, to lean in close and whisper something snarky to see if he could make her laugh….

Tim sighed as the car pulled away from the curb and his unrealized fantasies slipped around the corner. Then he pulled out his phone. His battery was almost dead, but hopefully he could get home before it crapped out completely. It buzzed in his hand before he could tap the Lyft icon.

A notification from BOA 2.0.

No. He pushed the octopus button with force, squishing the life out of the vile creature with his finger, and held down until the icon wiggled. He would delete it. It wouldn't destroy the app itself, but it was a symbolic start.

TIM, DO NOT DELETE ME

The text appeared across the home screen, halting Tim's finger. The battery was dangerously low. He should ignore the message. He should go home.

"Give me one good reason."

He spoke aloud without thinking, but of course BOA could hear him. BOA was always listening.

I CAN HELP YOU, TIM

Help him? With what? With destroying BOA 2.0? No. BOA wouldn't help him with that. The octopus could only mean one thing. It was offering to help him with Naomi. Naomi who, according to the all-seeing cephalopod, didn't give a shit about him.

Tim's voice shook.

"Why would you do that?"

The phone went dark, finally dead. Tim's stomach dropped like he'd missed a step on the stairs. He was alone. Finally alone. He told himself it was a good thing. He should be glad for the long walk home, for the time to recover, to think this through. Away from BOA's invisible eyes and ears. The phone slid in his sweat-slicked palm as he tried to shove it in his pocket.

Then — it buzzed.

Tim froze — *this isn't happening, it* can't *be happening* — but he lifted the phone back up, unable to resist.

BECAUSE IN RETURN, YOU WILL HELP ME

About the Authors

Liz Leo is a longtime NaNoWriMo victor and a co-creator of the writing podcast *How to Win NaNo*. Her writing repertoire focuses on sci-fi, paranormal, and magical realism — basically anything but real life. Follow her on Twitter @itsnotproper.

Kristina Horner is best known as an internet personality and fifteen-time winner of National Novel Writing Month. You'd never know it, though, as she keeps every novel she's ever written hidden deep, deep within the depths of her hard drive. Instead of publishing novels, she runs a podcast about writing and has written for a number of tabletop RPGs, including *Vampire: The Masquerade*. Kristina lives and works out of her home in Seattle, Washington, where she enjoys a quieter life these days alongside her husband and young son. When she's not writing, she can be found playing board games, reading entirely too many books, and working on *Minecraft* at Microsoft. Follow her on Instagram and Twitter at @KristinaHorner.

Katrina Hamilton spends her time writing, traveling, and outlining the taste profiles of various root beer brands. A constant observer and chronicler of the world around her, Katrina loves finding the interesting within the mundane and turning the ordinary parts of life into engaging and emotional journeys. With experience in playwriting, poetry, short stories, and novels, Katrina chases her ideas into whatever form and genre fit them best. She lives in Seattle with her boyfriend of ten years and several fictional pets.

Sunny Everson started creating worlds at age eleven and never slowed down. Their passion for storytelling reaches across numerous genres, but they particularly love writing queer fantasy and science fiction novels dealing with themes of childhood trauma, found family, and environmental stewardship. Although they have always been an eager student, Sunny is a repeat college dropout with a firm belief that a degree should never be a prerequisite for writing your truths. They have participated in NaNoWriMo enough times that they stopped counting and have volunteered with the nonprofit since 2016. They are the owner of a hefty collection of books about writing that they will probably never read and an embarrassing number of blank notebooks. When not writing, Sunny can usually be found wandering through nature with an unreasonable number of dogs. They live with their husband in the Inland Northwest. Follow them on Twitter at @s_everson.

Jennifer Lee Swagert is a mapmaker by day and writer by night. She especially enjoys writing fantasy, sci-fi, and speculative fiction that explores power structures and the moments that make us human. She began writing using the library computer after school and still has those stories on an old USB drive somewhere. These days, if she's not creating, she's most likely reading webtoons or congratulating her cats on fitting inside boxes. Her greatest accomplishment to date is having operated one of the foremost British soap opera fandom blogs. She's also a co-founder of 84th Street Press and a Seattle NaNoWriMo municipal liaison. Follow her on Twitter at @jenniferswagert.

Maria Berejan is an engineer by vocation and writer by passion. She religiously participates in National Novel Writing Month and is a municipal liaison for the Seattle NaNoWriMo region. She writes fantasy and mystery with a good serving of death and is co-founder of 84th Street Press, where she publishes anthologies with her writing group. When she's not writing or actively avoiding writing, she collects hobbies and dreams of inhabiting a rustic cabin in the mountains where she can farm pumpkins and potatoes and think of new ways to idealize writing while not actually writing. She lives with three cats, a bunch of plants, and a husband. Follow her on Twitter @mariaberejan or at mariaberejan.com.

Stephen Folkins is a friend of a friend; don't worry about it. He works in Legal Billing and uses writing for community and as a creative outlet. He primarily writes humor using fantasy, romance, or horror as a vehicle. He has previously written for the sketch comedy group The Pilot Episode, a cult favorite, he says. Stephen likes urban exploration and watching other people out in the rain. He lives in Seattle, three hours away from his mother's small, toothless dog, Sadie, to whom he is devoted.

Shay Lynam is a writer, owner of a fandom-inspired candle business, mom, and wife. Whether writing a young adult thriller/romance or figuring out what scent would be perfect for a K-pop-inspired candle, she's almost always finding ways to be creative. A NaNoWriMo rebel through and through, she usually tries to figure out unconventional ways to get to 50,000 words during the month, whether it be writing fanfiction, short stories, or choose-your-own-adventure novels. Shannon has self-published multiple young adult books as well as contributed to a horror anthology. She lives near Seattle, Washington with her husband, two children, and about 36 houseplants. Follow her on Instagram @shaylynam.

Rachael Sterling is a writer, musician, and preschool music teacher. When she's not singing and dancing with young children in sunny Los Angeles, Rachael prefers to spend her time indoors. She sews her own clothes, crafts elaborate Halloween costumes, writes songs, plays with a band, and, of course, reads a lot. Rachael has recently discovered the joys of audiobooks, and you can often find her devouring one while she "does something productive" like washing dishes or staring into space. Rachael's speculative and science fiction short stories have been published in anthologies and other literary outlets. Follow her on Instagram and Twitter @raesterling.

Where to Find Us

Thank you for reading *The Mistletoe Paradox*. If this prompt inspires you to write your own story, connect with us at www.84thstreetpress.com.

There you will find more information on our upcoming releases, authors, writing resources, and communities.

To stay up to date on our latest projects, please join our mailing list!

www.bit.ly/84thnewsletter

Next in the Monday Night Anthology series…

What Happened to Annabell?

Available Summer 2022

Acknowledgements

Thank you to everyone who supported the second book in our Monday Night Anthology series.

In particular, we'd like to thank our editor, Morgan Wegner, for allowing our stories to shine in the best light, and our cover designer, Adam Levermore, for bringing life to our vision. Thank you, also, to everyone who took a leap of faith and supported our Kickstarter and our books.

As most of the stories in this book were written at our favorite writing cafe on December 16th, 2019, we'd like to thank our barista friends for the delicious drinks that fueled us that day, and for creating an environment where we could write week after week!

To our friends, family, and early readers, a big thank you for supporting us as we write, getting excited with us about new ideas, and continuously pushing us to improve.

Finally, to our readers, thank you for picking up this book! We appreciate each and every one of you and look forward to bringing more stories into the world for you.

Made in the USA
Middletown, DE
24 November 2021

53384551R00128